INDIAN

By
CHARLES A. EASTMAN
(*Ohiyesa*)

A LETTER TO THE CHILDREN
DEAR CHILDREN:—You will like to know that the man who wrote these true stories is himself one of the people he describes so pleasantly and so lovingly for you. He hopes that when you have finished this book, the Indians will seem to you very real and very friendly. He is not willing that all your knowledge of the race that formerly possessed this continent should come from the lips of strangers and enemies, or that you should think of them as blood-thirsty and treacherous, as savage and unclean.

War, you know, is always cruel, and it is true that there were stern fighting men among the Indians, as well as among your own forefathers. But there were also men of peace, men generous and kindly and religious. There were tender mothers, and happy little ones, and a home life that was pure and true. There were high ideals of loyalty and honor. It will do you good and make you happier to read of these things.

Perhaps you wonder how a "real, live Indian" could write a book. I will tell you how. The story of this man's life is itself as wonderful as a fairy tale. Born in a wigwam, as he has told you, and early left motherless, he was brought up, like the little Hiawatha, by a good grandmother. When he was four years old, war broke out between his people and the United States government. The Indians were defeated and many of them were killed. Some fled northward into Canada and took refuge under the British flag, among them the writer of this book, with his grandmother and an uncle. His father was captured by the whites.

After ten years of that wild life, now everywhere at an end, of which he has given you a true picture in his books, his father, whom the good President Lincoln had pardoned and released from the military prison, made the long and dangerous journey to Canada to find and bring back his youngest son. The Sioux were beginning to learn that the old life must go, and that, if they were to survive at all, they must follow "the white man's road," long and hard as it looked to a free people. They were beginning to plow and sow and send their children to school.

Ohiyesa, the Winner, as the boy was called, came home with his father to what was then Dakota Territory, to a little settlement of Sioux homesteaders. Everything about the new life was strange to him, and at first he did not like it at all. He had thoughts of running away and making his way back to Canada. But his father, Many Lightnings, who had been baptized a Christian under the name of Jacob Eastman, told him that he, too, must take a new name, and he chose that of Charles Alexander Eastman. He was told to cut off his long hair and put on citizen's clothing. Then his father made him choose between going to school and working at the plow.

Ohiyesa tried plowing for half a day. It was hard work to break the tough prairie sod with his father's oxen and the strange implement they gave him. He decided to try school. Rather to his surprise, he liked it, and he kept on. His teachers were pleased with his progress, and soon better opportunities opened to him. He was sent farther east to a better school, where he continued to do well, and soon went higher. In the long summer vacations he worked, on farms, in shops and offices; and in winter he studied and played football and all the other games you play, until after about fifteen or sixteen years he found himself with the diplomas of a famous college and a great university, a Bachelor of Science, a Doctor of Medicine, and a doubly educated man—educated in the lore of the wilderness as well as in some of the deepest secrets of civilization.

Since that day, a good many more years have passed. Ohiyesa, known as Doctor Charles A. Eastman, has now a home and six children of his own among the New England hills. He has hundreds of devoted friends of both races. He is the author of five books which have been widely read, some of them in England, France and Germany as well as in America, and he speaks face to face to thousands of people every year. Perhaps some of you have heard from his own lips his recollections of wild life. You may find all the stories in this book, and many more of the same sort, in the books called "Indian Boyhood," and "Old Indian Days," published by Doubleday, Page and Company, of Garden City, L.I., who have kindly consented to the publication of this little volume in order that the children in our schools might read stories of real Indians by a real Indian.

CONTENTS
PART ONE
MY INDIAN CHILDHOOD

CHAPTER
I. "The Pitiful Last"
II. Early Hardships
III. An Indian Sugar Camp
IV. Games and Sports
V. An Indian Boy's Training
VI. The Boy Hunter
VII. Evening in the Lodge

PART TWO
STORIES OF REAL INDIANS

I. Winona's Childhood
II. Winona's Girlhood
III. A Midsummer Feast
IV. The Faithfulness of Long Ears
V. Snana's Fawn
VI. Hakadah's First Offering
VII. The Grave of the Dog

PART ONE
MY INDIAN CHILDHOOD
I
"THE PITIFUL LAST"

What boy would not be an Indian for a while when he thinks of the freest life in the world? This life was mine. Every day there was a real hunt. There was real game.

No people have a better use of their five senses than the children of the wilderness. We could smell as well as hear and see. We could feel and taste as well as we could see and hear. Nowhere has the memory been more fully developed than in the wild life, and I can still see wherein I owe much to my early training.

Of course I myself do not remember when I first saw the day, but my brothers have often recalled the event with much mirth; for it was a custom of the Sioux that when a boy was born his brother must plunge into the water, or roll in the snow naked if it was winter time; and if he was not big enough to do either of these himself, water was thrown on him. If the new-born had a sister, she must be immersed. The idea was that a warrior had come to camp, and the other children must display some act of hardihood.

I was so unfortunate as to be the youngest of five children who, soon after I was born, were left motherless. I had to bear the humiliating name "Hakādah," meaning "the pitiful last," until I should earn a more dignified and appropriate name. I was regarded as little more than a plaything by the rest of the children.

The babe was done up as usual in a movable cradle made from an oak board two and a half feet long and one and a half feet wide. On one side of it was nailed with brass-headed tacks the richly embroidered sack, which was open in front and laced up and down with buckskin strings. Over the arms of the infant was a wooden bow, the ends of which were firmly attached to the board, so that if the cradle should fall the child's head and face would be protected. On this bow were hung curious playthings—strings of artistically carved bones and hoofs of deer, which rattled when the little hands moved them.

In this upright cradle I lived, played, and slept the greater part of the time during the first few months of my life. Whether I was made to lean against a lodge pole or was suspended from a bough of a tree, while my grandmother cut wood, or whether I was carried on her back, or conveniently balanced by another child in a similar cradle hung on the opposite side of a pony, I was still in my oaken bed.

This grandmother, who had already lived through sixty years of hardships, was a wonder to the young maidens of the tribe. She showed no less enthusiasm over Hakadah than she had done when she held her first-born, the boy's father, in her arms. Every little attention that is due to a loved child she performed with much skill and devotion. She made all my scanty garments and my tiny moccasins with a great deal of taste. It was said by all that I could not have had more attention had my mother been living.

Uncheedah (grandmother) was a great singer. Sometimes, when Hakadah wakened too early in the morning, she would sing to him something like the following lullaby:

Sleep, sleep, my boy, the Chippewas
Are far away—are far away.
Sleep, sleep, my boy; prepare to meet
The foe by day—the foe by day!
The cowards will not dare to fight
Till morning break—till morning break.
Sleep, sleep, my child, while still 'tis night;
Then bravely wake—then bravely wake!

The Dakota women were wont to cut and bring their fuel from the woods and, in fact, to perform most of the drudgery of the camp. This of necessity fell to their lot because the men must follow the game during the day. Very often my grandmother carried me with her on these excursions; and while she worked it was her habit to suspend me from a wild grape vine or a springy bough, so that the least breeze would swing the cradle to and fro.

She has told me that when I had grown old enough to take notice, I was apparently capable of holding extended conversations in an unknown dialect with birds and red squirrels. Once I fell asleep in my cradle, suspended five or six feet from the ground, while Uncheedah was some distance away, gathering birch bark for a canoe. A squirrel had found it convenient to come upon the bow of my cradle and nibble his hickory nut, until he awoke me by dropping the crumbs of his meal. It was a common thing for birds to alight on my cradle in the woods.

After I left my cradle, I almost walked away from it, she told me. She then began calling my attention to natural objects. Whenever I heard the song of a bird, she would tell me what bird it came from, something after this fashion:

"Hakadah, listen to Shechoka (the robin) calling his mate. He says he has just found something good to eat." Or "Listen to Oopehanska (the thrush); he is singing for his little wife. He will sing his best." When in the evening the whippoorwill started his song with vim, no further than a stone's throw from our tent in the woods, she would say to me:

"Hush! It may be an Ojibway scout!"

Again, when I waked at midnight, she would say:
"Do not cry! Hinakaga (the owl) is watching you from the tree-top."
I usually covered up my head, for I had perfect faith in my grandmother's admonitions, and she had given me a dreadful idea of this bird. It was one of her legends that a little boy was once standing just outside of the teepee (tent), crying vigorously for his mother, when Hinakaga swooped down in the darkness and carried the poor little fellow up into the trees. It was well known that the hoot of the owl was commonly imitated by Indian scouts when on the war-path. There had been dreadful massacres immediately following this call. Therefore it was deemed wise to impress the sound early upon the mind of the child.

Indian children were trained so that they hardly ever cried much in the night. This was very expedient and necessary in their exposed life. In my infancy it was my grandmother's custom to put me to sleep, as she said, with the birds, and to waken me with them, until it became a habit. She did this with an object in view. An Indian must always rise early. In the first place, as a hunter, he finds his game best at daybreak. Secondly, other tribes, when on the war-path, usually make their attack very early in the morning. Even when our people are moving about leisurely, we like to rise before daybreak, in order to travel when the air is cool, and unobserved, perchance, by our enemies.

As a little child, it was instilled into me to be silent and reticent. This was one of the most important traits to form in the character of the Indian. As a hunter and warrior it was considered absolutely necessary to him, and was thought to lay the foundations of patience and self-control.

II
EARLY HARDSHIPS

One of the earliest recollections of my adventurous childhood is the ride I had on a pony's side. I was passive in the whole matter. A little girl cousin of mine was put in a bag and suspended from the horn of an Indian saddle; but her weight must be balanced or the saddle would not remain on the animal's back. Accordingly, I was put into another sack and made to keep the saddle and the girl in position! I did not object, for I had a very pleasant game of peek-a-boo with the little girl, until we came to a big snow-drift, where the poor beast was stuck fast and began to lie down. Then it was not so nice!

This was the convenient and primitive way in which some mothers packed their children for winter journeys. However cold the weather might be, the inmate of the fur-lined sack was usually very comfortable—at least I used to think so. I believe I was accustomed to all the precarious Indian conveyances, and, as a boy, I enjoyed the dog-travaux ride as much as any. The travaux consisted of a set of rawhide strips securely lashed to the tent-poles, which were harnessed to the sides of the animal as if he stood between shafts, while the free ends were allowed to drag on the ground. Both ponies and large dogs were used as beasts of burden, and they carried in this way the smaller children as well as the baggage.

This mode of travelling for children was possible only in the summer, and as the dogs were sometimes unreliable, the little ones were exposed to a certain amount of danger. For instance, whenever a train of dogs had been travelling for a long time, almost perishing with the heat and their heavy loads, a glimpse of water would cause them to forget all their responsibilities. Some of them, in spite of the screams of the women, would swim with their burdens into the cooling stream, and I was thus, on more than one occasion, made to partake of an unwilling bath.

I was a little over four years old at the time of the "Sioux massacre" in Minnesota. In the general turmoil, we took flight into British Columbia, and the journey is still vividly remembered by all our family. A yoke of oxen and a lumber-wagon were taken from some white farmer and brought home for our conveyance.

How delighted I was when I learned that we were to ride behind those wise-looking animals and in that gorgeously painted wagon! It seemed almost like a living creature to me, this new vehicle with four legs, and the more so when we got out of axle-grease and the wheels went along squealing like pigs!

The boys found a great deal of innocent fun in jumping from the high wagon while the oxen were leisurely moving along. My elder brothers soon became experts. At last, I mustered up courage enough to join them in this sport. I was sure they stepped on the wheel, so I cautiously placed my moccasined foot upon it. Alas, before I could realize what had happened, I was under the wheels, and had it not been for the neighbor immediately behind us, I might have been run over by the next team as well.

This was my first experience with a civilized vehicle. I cried out all possible reproaches on the white man's team and concluded that a dog-travaux was good enough for me. I was really rejoiced that we were moving away from the people who made the wagon that had almost ended my life, and it did not occur to me that I alone was to blame. I could not be persuaded to ride in that wagon again and was glad when we finally left it beside the Missouri river.

The summer after the "Minnesota massacre," General Sibley pursued our people across this river. Now the Missouri is considered one of the most treacherous rivers in the world. Even a good modern boat is not safe upon its uncertain current. We were forced to cross in buffalo-skin boats—as round as tubs!

The Washechu (white men) were coming in great numbers with their big guns, and while most of our men were fighting them to gain time, the women and the old men made and equipped the temporary boats, braced with ribs of willow. Some of these were towed by two or three women or men swimming in the water and some by ponies. It was not an easy matter to keep them right side up, with their helpless freight of little children and such goods as we possessed.

In our flight, we little folks were strapped in the saddles or held in front of an older person, and in the long night marches to get away from the soldiers, we suffered from loss of sleep and insufficient food. Our meals were eaten hastily, and sometimes in the saddle. Water was not always to be found. The people carried it with them in bags formed of tripe or the dried pericardium of animals.

Now we were compelled to trespass upon the country of hostile tribes and were harassed by them almost daily and nightly. Only the strictest vigilance saved us.

One day we met with another enemy near the British lines. It was a prairie fire. We were surrounded. Another fire was quickly made, which saved our lives.

One of the most thrilling experiences of the following winter was a blizzard, which overtook us in our wanderings. Here and there, a family lay down in the snow, selecting a place where it was not likely to drift much. For a day and a night we lay under the snow. Uncle stuck a long pole beside us to tell us when the storm was over. We had plenty of buffalo robes and the snow kept us warm, but we found it heavy. After a time, it became packed and hollowed out around our bodies, so that we were as comfortable as one can be under those circumstances.

The next day the storm ceased, and we discovered a large herd of buffaloes almost upon us. We dug our way out, shot some of the buffaloes, made a fire and enjoyed a good dinner.

I was now an exile as well as motherless; yet I was not unhappy. Our wanderings from place to place afforded us many pleasant experiences and quite as many hardships and misfortunes. There were times of plenty and times of scarcity, and we had several narrow escapes from death. In savage life, the early spring is the most trying time and almost all the famines occurred at this period of the year.

The Indians are a patient and a clannish people; their love for one another is stronger than that of any civilized people I know. If this were not so, I believe there would have been tribes of cannibals among them. White people have been known to kill and eat their companions in preference to starving; but Indians—never!

In times of famine, the adults often denied themselves in order to make the food last as long as possible for the children, who were not able to bear hunger as well as the old. As a people, they can live without food much longer than any other nation.

I once passed through one of these hard springs when we had nothing to eat for several days. I well remember the six small birds which constituted the breakfast for six families one morning; and then we had no dinner or supper to follow! What a relief that was to me—although I had only a small wing of a small bird for my share! Soon after this, we came into a region where buffaloes were plenty, and hunger and scarcity were forgotten.

Such was the Indians' wild life! When game was to be had and the sun shone, they easily forgot the bitter experiences of the winter before. Little preparation was made for the future. They are children of Nature, and occasionally she whips them with the lashes of experience, yet they are forgetful and careless. Much of their suffering might have been prevented by a little calculation.

During the summer, when Nature is at her best, and provides abundantly for the savage, it seems to me that no life is happier than his! Food is free—lodging free—everything free! All were alike rich in the summer, and, again, all were alike poor in the winter and early spring. However, their diseases were fewer and not so destructive as now, and the Indian's health was generally good. The Indian boy enjoyed such a life as almost all boys dream of and would choose for themselves if they were permitted to do so.

The raids made upon our people by other tribes were frequent, and we had to be constantly on the watch. I remember at one time a night attack was made upon our camp and all our ponies stampeded. Only a few of them were recovered, and our journeys after this misfortune were effected mostly by means of the dog-travaux.

The second winter after the massacre, my father and my two older brothers, with several others, were betrayed by a half-breed at Winnipeg to the United States authorities. As I was then living with my uncle in another part of the country, I became separated from them for ten years. During all this time we believed that they had been killed by the whites, and I was taught that I must avenge their deaths as soon as I was able to go upon the war-path.

III
AN INDIAN SUGAR CAMP

With the first March thaw the thoughts of the Indian women of my childhood days turned promptly to the annual sugar-making. This industry was chiefly followed by the old men and women and the children. The rest of the tribe went out upon the spring fur-hunt at this season, leaving us at home to make the sugar.

The first and most important of the necessary utensils were the huge iron and brass kettles for boiling. Everything else could be made, but these must be bought, begged or borrowed. A maple tree was felled and a log canoe hollowed out, into which the sap was to be gathered. Little troughs of basswood and birchen basins were also made to receive the sweet drops as they trickled from the tree.

As soon as these labors were accomplished, we all proceeded to the bark sugar house, which stood in the midst of a fine grove of maples on the bank of the Minnesota river. We found this hut partially filled with the snows of winter and the withered leaves of the preceding autumn, and it must be cleared for our use. In the meantime a tent was pitched outside for a few days' occupancy. The snow was still deep in the woods, with a solid crust upon which we could easily walk; for we usually moved to the sugar house before the sap had actually started, the better to complete our preparations.

My grandmother did not confine herself to canoe-making. She also collected a good supply of fuel for the fires, for she would not have much time to gather wood when the sap began to flow. Presently the weather moderated and the snow began to melt. The month of April brought showers which carried most of it off into the Minnesota river. Now the women began to test the trees—moving leisurely among them, axe in hand, and striking a single quick blow, to see if the sap would appear. Trees, like people, have their individual characters; some were ready to yield up their life-blood, while others were more reluctant. Now one of the birchen basins was set under each tree, and a hardwood chip driven deep into the cut which the axe had made. From the corners of this chip—at first drop by drop, then, more freely—the sap trickled into the little dishes.

It is usual to make sugar from maples, but several other trees were also tapped by the Indians. From the birch and ash was made a dark-colored sugar, with a somewhat bitter taste, which was used for medicinal purposes. The box-elder yielded a beautiful white sugar, whose only fault was that there was never enough of it!

A long fire was now made in the sugar house, and a row of brass kettles suspended over the blaze. The sap was collected by the women in tin or birchen buckets and poured into the canoes, from which the kettles were kept filled. The hearts of the boys beat high with pleasant anticipations when they heard the welcome hissing sound of the boiling sap! Each boy claimed one kettle for his especial charge. It was his duty to see that the fire was kept under it, to watch lest it boil over, and finally, when the sap became sirup, to test it upon the snow, dipping it out with a wooden paddle. So frequent were these tests that for the first day or two we consumed nearly all that could be made; and it was not until the sweetness began to pall that my grandmother set herself in earnest to store up sugar for future use. She made it into cakes of various forms, in birchen molds, and sometimes in hollow canes or reeds, and the bills of ducks and geese. Some of it was pulverized and packed in rawhide cases. Being a prudent woman, she did not give it to us after the first month or so, except upon special occasions, and it was thus made to last almost the year around. The smaller candies were reserved as an occasional treat for the little fellows, and the sugar was eaten at feasts with wild rice or parched corn, and also with pounded dried meat. Coffee and tea, with their substitutes, were all unknown to us in those days.

Every pursuit has its trials and anxieties. My grandmother's special tribulations, during the sugaring season, were the upsetting and gnawing of holes in her birch-bark pans. The transgressors were the rabbit and squirrel tribes, and we little boys for once became useful, in shooting them with our bows and arrows. We hunted all over the sugar camp, until the little creatures were fairly driven out of the neighborhood. Occasionally one of my older brothers brought home a rabbit or two, and then we had a feast.

I remember on this occasion of our last sugar bush in Minnesota, that I stood one day outside of our hut and watched the approach of a visitor— a bent old man, his hair almost white, and carrying on his back a large bundle of red willow, or kinnikinick, which the Indians use for smoking. He threw down his load at the door and thus saluted us: "You have indeed perfect weather for sugar-making."

It was my great-grandfather, Cloud Man, whose original village was on the shores of Lakes Calhoun and Harriet, now in the suburbs of the city of Minneapolis. He was the first Sioux chief to welcome the Protestant missionaries among his people, and a well-known character in those pioneer days. He brought us word that some of the peaceful sugar-makers near us on the river had been attacked and murdered by roving Ojibways. This news disturbed us not a little, for we realized that we too might become the victims of an Ojibway war party. Therefore we all felt some uneasiness from this time until we returned heavy laden to our village.

IV
GAMES AND SPORTS

The Indian boy was a prince of the wilderness. He had but very little work to do during the period of his boyhood. His principal occupation was the practice of a few simple arts in warfare and the chase. Aside from this, he was master of his time.

It is true that our savage life was a precarious one, and full of dreadful catastrophes; however, this never prevented us from enjoying our sports to the fullest extent. As we left our teepees in the morning, we were never sure that our scalps would not dangle from a pole in the afternoon! It was an uncertain life, to be sure. Yet we observed that the fawns skipped and played happily while the gray wolves might be peeping forth from behind the hills, ready to tear them limb from limb.

Our sports were molded by the life and customs of our people; indeed, we practiced only what we expected to do when grown. Our games were feats with the bow and arrow, foot and pony races, wrestling, swimming and imitation of the customs and habits of our fathers. We had sham fights with mud balls and willow wands; we played lacrosse, made war upon bees, shot winter arrows (which were used only in that season), and coasted upon the ribs of animals and buffalo robes.

No sooner did the boys get together than, as a usual thing, they divided into squads and chose sides; then a leading arrow was shot at random into the air. Before it fell to the ground a volley from the bows of the participants followed. Each player was quick to note the direction and speed of the leading arrow and he tried to send his own at the same speed and at an equal height, so that when it fell it would be closer to the first than any of the others.

It was considered out of place to shoot by first sighting the object aimed at. This was usually impracticable in actual life, because the object was almost always in motion, while the hunter himself was often upon the back of a pony at full gallop. Therefore, it was the off-hand shot that the Indian boy sought to master. There was another game with arrows that was characterized by gambling, and was generally confined to the men.

The races were an every-day occurrence. At noon the boys were usually gathered by some pleasant sheet of water, and as soon as the ponies were watered, they were allowed to graze for an hour or two, while the boys stripped for their noonday sports. A boy might say to some other whom he considered his equal:

"I can't run; but I will challenge you to fifty paces."

A former hero, when beaten, would often explain his defeat by saying: "I drank too much water."

Boys of all ages were paired for a "spin," and the little red men cheered on their favorites with spirit.

As soon as this was ended, the pony races followed. All the speedy ponies were picked out and riders chosen. If a boy declined to ride, there would be shouts of derision.

Last of all came the swimming. A little urchin would hang to his pony's long tail, while the latter, with only his head above water, glided sportively along. Finally the animals were driven into a fine field of grass and we turned our attention to other games.

The "mud-and-willow" fight was rather a severe and dangerous sport. A lump of soft clay was stuck on the end of a limber and springy willow wand and thrown as boys throw apples from sticks, with considerable force. When there were fifty or a hundred players on each side, the battle became warm; but anything to arouse the bravery of Indian boys seemed to them a good and wholesome diversion.

Wrestling was largely indulged in by us all. It may seem odd, but wrestling was done by a great many boys at once—from ten to any number on a side. It was really a battle, in which each one chose his opponent. The rule was that if a boy sat down, he was let alone, but as long as he remained standing within the field, he was open to an attack. No one struck with the hand, but all manner of tripping with legs and feet and butting with the knees was allowed. Altogether it was an exhausting pastime—fully equal to the American game of football, and only the young athlete could really enjoy it.

One of our most curious sports was a war upon the nests of wild bees. We imagined ourselves about to make an attack upon the Ojibways or some tribal foe. We all painted and stole cautiously upon the nest; then, with a rush and war-whoop, sprang upon the object of our attack and endeavored to destroy it. But it seemed that the bees were always on the alert and never entirely surprised, for they always raised quite as many scalps as did their bold assailants! After the onslaught upon the nest was ended, we usually followed it by a pretended scalp dance.

On the occasion of my first experience in this mode of warfare, there were two other little boys who were also novices. One of them particularly was really too young to indulge in an exploit of that kind. As it was the custom of our people, when they killed or wounded an enemy on the battle-field, to announce the act in a loud voice, we did the same. My friend, Little Wound (as I will call him, for I do not remember his name), being quite small, was unable to reach the nest until it had been well trampled upon and broken and the insects had made a counter charge with such vigor as to repulse and scatter our numbers in every direction. However, he evidently did not want to retreat without any honors; so he bravely jumped upon the nest and yelled:

"I, the brave Little Wound, to-day kill the only fierce enemy!"

Scarcely were the last words uttered when he screamed as if stabbed to the heart. One of his older companions shouted:

"Dive into the water! Run! Dive into the water!" for there was a lake near by. This advice he obeyed.

When we had reassembled and were indulging in our mimic dance, Little Wound was not allowed to dance. He was considered not to be in existence—he had been killed by our enemies, the Bee tribe. Poor little fellow! His swollen face was sad and ashamed as he sat on a fallen log and watched the dance. Although he might well have styled himself one of the noble dead who had died for their country, yet he was not unmindful that he had *screamed*, and this weakness would be apt to recur to him many times in the future.

We had some quiet plays which we alternated with the more severe and warlike ones. Among them were throwing wands and snow-arrows. In the winter we coasted much. We had no "double-rippers" or toboggans, but six or seven of the long ribs of a buffalo, fastened together at the larger end, answered all practical purposes. Sometimes a strip of basswood bark, four feet long and about six inches wide, was used with considerable skill. We stood on one end and held the other, using the slippery inside of the bark for the outside, and thus coasting down long hills with remarkable speed.

The spinning of tops was one of the all-absorbing winter sports. We made our tops heart-shaped of wood, horn or bone. We whipped them with a long thong of buckskin. The handle was a stick about a foot long and sometimes we whittled the stick to make it spoon-shaped at one end.

We played games with these tops—two to fifty boys at one time. Each whips his top until it hums; then one takes the lead and the rest follow in a sort of obstacle race. The top must spin all the way through. There were bars of snow over which we must pilot our top in the spoon end of our whip; then again we would toss it in the air on to another open spot of ice or smooth snow-crust from twenty to fifty paces away. The top that holds out the longest is the winner.

We loved to play in the water. When we had no ponies, we often had swimming matches of our own, and sometimes made rafts with which we crossed lakes and rivers. It was a common thing to "duck" a young or timid boy or to carry him into deep water to struggle as best he might.

I remember a perilous ride with a companion on an unmanageable log, when we were both less than seven years old. The older boys had put us on this uncertain bark and pushed us out into the swift current of the river. I cannot speak for my comrade in distress, but I can say now that I would rather ride on a swift bronco any day than try to stay on and steady a short log in a river. I never knew how we managed to prevent a shipwreck on that voyage and to reach the shore.

We had many curious wild pets. There were young foxes, bears, wolves, raccoons, fawns, buffalo calves and birds of all kinds, tamed by various boys. My pets were different at different times, but I particularly remember one. I once had a grizzly bear for a pet, and so far as he and I were concerned, our relations were charming and very close. But I hardly know whether he made more enemies for me or I for him. It was his habit to treat every boy unmercifully who injured me.

V
AN INDIAN BOY'S TRAINING

Very early, the Indian boy assumed the task of preserving and transmitting the legends of his ancestors and his race. Almost every evening a myth, or a true story of some deed done in the past, was narrated by one of the parents or grand-parents, while the boy listened with parted lips and glistening eyes. On the following evening, he was usually required to repeat it. If he was not an apt scholar, he struggled long with his task; but, as a rule, the Indian boy is a good listener and has a good memory, so that the stories were tolerably well mastered. The household became his audience, by which he was alternately criticized and applauded.

This sort of teaching at once enlightens the boy's mind and stimulates his ambition. His conception of his own future career becomes a vivid and irresistible force. Whatever there is for him to learn must be learned; whatever qualifications are necessary to a truly great man he must seek at any expense of danger and hardship. Such was the feeling of the imaginative and brave young Indian. It became apparent to him in early life that he must accustom himself to rove alone and not to fear or dislike the impression of solitude.

It seems to be a popular idea that all the characteristic skill of the Indian is instinctive and hereditary. This is a mistake. All the stoicism and patience of the Indian are acquired traits, and continual practice alone makes him master of the art of wood-craft. Physical training and dieting were not neglected. I remember that I was not allowed to have beef soup or any warm drink. The soup was for the old men. General rules for the young were never to take their food very hot, nor to drink much water.

My uncle, who educated me up to the age of fifteen years, was a strict disciplinarian and a good teacher. When I left the teepee in the morning, he would say: "Hakadah, look closely to everything you see"; and at evening, on my return, he used often to catechize me for an hour or so.

"On which side of the trees is the lighter-colored bark? On which side do they have most regular branches?"

It was his custom to let me name all the new birds that I had seen during the day. I would name them according to the color or the shape of the bill or their song or the appearance and locality of the nest—in fact, anything about the bird that impressed me as characteristic. I made many ridiculous errors, I must admit. He then usually informed me of the correct name. Occasionally I made a hit and this he would warmly commend.

He went much deeper into this science when I was a little older, that is, about the age of eight or nine years. He would say, for instance:

"How do you know that there are fish in yonder lake?"

"Because they jump out of the water for flies at mid-day."

He would smile at my prompt but superficial reply.

"What do you think of the little pebbles grouped together under the shallow water? and what made the pretty curved marks in the sandy bottom and the little sand-banks? Where do you find the fish-eating birds? Have the inlet and the outlet of a lake anything to do with the question?"

He did not expect a correct reply at once to all the questions that he put to me on these occasions, but he meant to make me observant and a good student of nature.

"Hakadah," he would say to me, "you ought to follow the example of the shunktokecha (wolf). Even when he is surprised and runs for his life, he will pause to take one more look at you before he enters his final retreat. So you must take a second look at everything you see.

"It is better to view animals unobserved. I have been a witness to their courtships and their quarrels and have learned many of their secrets in this way. I was once the unseen spectator of a thrilling battle between a pair of grizzly bears and three buffaloes—a rash act for the bears, for it was in the moon of strawberries, when the buffaloes sharpen and polish their horns for bloody contests among themselves.

"I advise you, my boy, never to approach a grizzly's den from the front, but to steal up behind and throw your blanket or a stone in front of the hole. He does not usually rush for it, but first puts his head out and listens and then comes out very indifferently and sits on his haunches on the mound in front of the hole before he makes any attack. While he is exposing himself in this fashion, aim at his heart. Always be as cool as the animal himself." Thus he armed me against the cunning of savage beasts by teaching me how to outwit them.

"In hunting," he would resume, "you will be guided by the habits of the animal you seek. Remember that a moose stays in swampy or low land or between high mountains near a spring or lake, for thirty to sixty days at a time. Most large game moves about continually, except the doe in the spring; it is then a very easy matter to find her with the fawn. Conceal yourself in a convenient place as soon as you observe any signs of the presence of either, and then call with your birchen doe-caller.

"Whichever one hears you first will soon appear in your neighborhood. But you must be very watchful, or you may be made a fawn of by a large wild-cat. They understand the characteristic call of the doe perfectly well.

"When you have any difficulty with a bear or a wild-cat—that is, if the creature shows any signs of attacking you—you must make him fully understand that you have seen him and are aware of his intentions. If you are not well equipped for a pitched battle, the only way to make him retreat is to take a long sharp-pointed pole for a spear and rush toward him. No wild beast will face this unless he is cornered and already wounded. These fierce beasts are generally afraid of the common weapon of the larger animals,—the horns,—and if these are very long and sharp, they dare not risk an open fight.

"There is one exception to this rule—the gray wolf will attack fiercely when very hungry. But their courage depends upon their numbers; in this they are like white men. One wolf or two will never attack a man. They will stampede a herd of buffaloes in order to get at the calves; they will rush upon a herd of antelopes, for these are helpless; but they are always careful about attacking man."

Of this nature were the instructions of my uncle, who was widely known at that time as among the greatest hunters of his tribe.

All boys were expected to endure hardship without complaint. In savage warfare, a young man must, of course, be an athlete and used to undergoing all sorts of privations. He must be able to go without food and water for two or three days without displaying any weakness, or to run for a day and a night without any rest. He must be able to traverse a pathless and wild country without losing his way either in the day or night time. He cannot refuse to do any of these things if he aspires to be a warrior.

Sometimes my uncle would waken me very early in the morning and challenge me to fast with him all day. I had to accept the challenge. We blackened our faces with charcoal, so that every boy in the village would know that I was fasting for the day. Then the little tempters would make my life a misery until the merciful sun hid behind the western hills.

I can scarcely recall the time when my stern teacher began to give sudden war-whoops over my head in the morning while I was sound asleep. He expected me to leap up with perfect presence of mind, always ready to grasp a weapon of some sort and to give a shrill whoop in reply. If I was sleepy or startled and hardly knew what I was about, he would ridicule me and say that I need never expect to sell my scalp dear. Often he would vary these tactics by shooting off his gun just outside of the lodge while I was yet asleep, at the same time giving blood-curdling yells. After a time I became used to this.

When Indians went upon the war-path, it was their custom to try the new warriors thoroughly before coming to an engagement. For instance, when they were near a hostile camp, they would select the novices to go after the water and make them do all sorts of things to prove their courage. In accordance with this idea, my uncle used to send me off after water when we camped after dark in a strange place. Perhaps the country was full of wild beasts, and, for aught I knew, there might be scouts from hostile bands of Indians lurking in that very neighborhood.

Yet I never objected, for that would show cowardice. I picked my way through the woods, dipped my pail in the water and hurried back, always careful to make as little noise as a cat. Being only a boy, my heart would leap at every crackling of a dry twig or distant hooting of an owl, until, at last, I reached our teepee. Then my uncle would perhaps say: "Ah, Hakadah, you are a thorough warrior!" empty out the precious contents of the pail, and order me to go a second time.

Imagine how I felt! But I wished to be a brave man as much as a white boy desires to be a great lawyer or even President of the United States. Silently I would take the pail and endeavor to retrace my foot-steps in the dark.

With all this, our manners and morals were not neglected. I was made to respect the adults and especially the aged. I was not allowed to join in their discussions, nor even to speak in their presence, unless requested to do so. Indian etiquette was very strict, and among the requirements was that of avoiding the direct address. A term of relationship or some title of courtesy was commonly used instead of the personal name by those who wished to show respect. We were taught generosity to the poor and reverence for the "Great Mystery." Religion was the basis of all Indian training.

VI
THE BOY HUNTER

There was almost as much difference between the Indian boys who were brought up on the open prairies and those of the woods, as between city and country boys. The hunting of the prairie boys was limited and their knowledge of natural history imperfect. They were, as a rule, good riders, but in all-round physical development much inferior to the red men of the forest.

Our hunting varied with the season of the year, and the nature of the country which was for the time our home. Our chief weapon was the bow and arrows, and perhaps, if we were lucky, a knife was possessed by some one in the crowd. In the olden times, knives and hatchets were made from bone and sharp stones.

For fire we used a flint with a spongy piece of dry wood and a stone to strike with. Another way of starting fire was for several of the boys to sit down in a circle and rub two pieces of dry, spongy wood together, one after another, until the wood took fire.

We hunted in company a great deal, though it was a common thing for a boy to set out for the woods quite alone, and he usually enjoyed himself fully as much. Our game consisted mainly of small birds, rabbits, squirrels and grouse. Fishing, too, occupied much of our time. We hardly ever passed a creek or a pond without searching for some signs of fish. When fish were present, we always managed to get some. Fish-lines were made of wild hemp, sinew or horse-hair. We either caught fish with lines, snared or speared them, or shot them with bow and arrows. In the fall we charmed them up to the surface by gently tickling them with a stick and quickly threw them out. We have sometimes dammed the brooks and driven the larger fish into a willow basket made for that purpose.

It was part of our hunting to find new and strange things in the woods. We examined the slightest sign of life; and if a bird had scratched the leaves off the ground, or a bear dragged up a root for his morning meal, we stopped to speculate on the time it was done. If we saw a large old tree with some scratches on its bark, we concluded that a bear or some raccoons must be living there. In that case we did not go any nearer than was necessary, but later reported the incident at home. An old deer-track would at once bring on a warm discussion as to whether it was the track of a buck or a doe. Generally, at noon, we met and compared our game, noting at the same time the peculiar characteristics of everything we had killed. It was not merely a hunt, for we combined with it the study of animal life. We also kept strict account of our game, and thus learned who were the best shots among the boys.

I am sorry to say that we were merciless toward the birds. We often took their eggs and their young ones. My brother Chatanna and I once had a disagreeable adventure while bird-hunting. We were accustomed to catch in our hands young ducks and geese during the summer, and while doing this we happened to find a crane's nest. Of course, we were delighted with our good luck. But, as it was already midsummer, the young cranes—two in number—were rather large and they were a little way from the nest; we also observed that the two old cranes were in a swampy place near by; but, as it was moulting-time, we did not suppose that they would venture on dry land. So we proceeded to chase the young birds; but they were fleet runners and it took us some time to come up with them.

Meanwhile, the parent birds had heard the cries of their little ones and come to their rescue. They were chasing us, while we followed the birds. It was really a perilous encounter! Our strong bows finally gained the victory in a hand-to-hand struggle with the angry cranes; but after that we hardly ever hunted a crane's nest. Almost all birds make some resistance when their eggs or young are taken, but they will seldom attack man fearlessly.

We used to climb large trees for birds of all kinds; but we never undertook to get young owls unless they were on the ground. The hooting owl especially is a dangerous bird to attack under these circumstances.

I was once trying to catch a yellow-winged woodpecker in its nest when my arm became twisted and lodged in the deep hole so that I could not get it out without the aid of a knife; but we were a long way from home and my only companion was a deaf-mute cousin of mine. I was about fifty feet up in the tree, in a very uncomfortable position, but I had to wait there for more than an hour before he brought me the knife with which I finally released myself.

Our devices for trapping small animals were rude, but they were often successful. For instance, we used to gather up a peck or so of large, sharp-pointed burrs and scatter them in the rabbit's furrow-like path. In the morning, we would find the little fellow sitting quietly in his tracks, unable to move, for the burrs stuck to his feet.

Another way of snaring rabbits and grouse was the following: We made nooses of twisted horse-hair, which we tied very firmly to the top of a limber young tree, then bent the latter down to the track and fastened the whole with a slip-knot, after adjusting the noose. When the rabbit runs his head through the noose, he pulls the slip-knot and is quickly carried up by the spring of the young tree. This is a good plan, for the rabbit is out of harm's way as he swings high in the air.

Perhaps the most enjoyable of all was the chipmunk hunt. We killed these animals at any time of year, but the special time to hunt them was in March. After the first thaw, the chipmunks burrow a hole through the snow crust and make their first appearance for the season. Sometimes as many as fifty will come together and hold a social reunion. These gatherings occur early in the morning, from daybreak to about nine o'clock.

We boys learned this, among other secrets of nature, and got our blunt-headed arrows together in good season for the chipmunk expedition.

We generally went in groups of six to a dozen or fifteen, to see which would get the most. On the evening before, we selected several boys who could imitate the chipmunk's call with wild oat-straws and each of these provided himself with a supply of straws.

The crust will hold the boys nicely at this time of the year. Bright and early, they all come together at the appointed place, from which each group starts out in a different direction, agreeing to meet somewhere at a given position of the sun.

My first experience of this kind is still well remembered. It was a fine crisp March morning, and the sun had not yet shown himself among the distant tree-tops as we hurried along through the ghostly wood. Presently we arrived at a place where there were many signs of the animals. Then each of us selected a tree and took up his position behind it. The chipmunk-caller sat upon a log as motionless as he could, and began to call.

Soon we heard the patter of little feet on the hard snow; then we saw the chipmunks approaching from all directions. Some stopped and ran experimentally up a tree or a log, as if uncertain of the exact direction of the call; others chased one another about.

In a few minutes, the chipmunk-caller was besieged with them. Some ran all over his person, others under him and still others ran up the tree against which he was sitting. Each boy remained immovable until their leader gave the signal; then a great shout arose, and the chipmunks in their flight all ran up the different trees.

Now the shooting-match began. The little creatures seemed to realize their hopeless position; they would try again and again to come down the trees and flee away from the deadly aim of the youthful hunters. But they were shot down very fast; and whenever several of them rushed toward the ground, the little redskin hugged the tree and yelled frantically to scare them up again.

Each boy shoots always against the trunk of the tree, so that the arrow may bound back to him every time; otherwise, when he had shot away all of them, he would be helpless, and another, who had cleared his own tree, would come and take away his game, so there was warm competition. Sometimes a desperate chipmunk would jump from the top of the tree in order to escape, which was considered a joke on the boy who lost it and a triumph for the brave little animal. At last all were killed or gone, and then we went on to another place, keeping up the sport until the sun came out and the chipmunks refused to answer the call.

VII
EVENING IN THE LODGE

I had been skating on that part of the lake where there was an overflow, and came home somewhat cold. I cannot say just how cold it was, but it must have been intensely so, for the trees were cracking all about me like pistol-shots. I did not mind, because I was wrapped up in my buffalo robe with the hair inside, and a wide leather belt held it about my loins. My skates were nothing more than strips of basswood bark bound upon my feet.

I had taken off my frozen moccasins and put on dry ones in their places.

"Where have you been and what have you been doing?" Uncheedah asked as she placed before me some roast venison in a wooden bowl. "Did you see any tracks of moose or bear?"

"No, grandmother, I have only been playing at the lower end of the lake. I have something to ask you," I said, eating my dinner and supper together with all the relish of a hungry boy who has been skating in the cold for half a day.

"I found this feather, grandmother, and I could not make out what tribe wear feathers in that shape."

"Ugh, I am not a man; you had better ask your uncle. Besides, you should know it yourself by this time. You are now old enough to think about eagle feathers."

I felt mortified by this reminder of my ignorance. It seemed a reflection on me that I was not ambitious enough to have found all such matters out before.

"Uncle, you will tell me, won't you?" I said, in an appealing tone.

"I am surprised, my boy, that you should fail to recognize this feather. It is a Cree medicine feather, and not a warrior's."

"Then," I said, with much embarrassment, "you had better tell me again, uncle, the language of the feathers. I have really forgotten it all."

The day was now gone; the moon had risen; but the cold had not lessened, for the trunks of the trees were still snapping all around our teepee, which was lighted and warmed by the immense logs which Uncheedah's industry had provided. My uncle, White Footprint, now undertook to explain to me the significance of the eagle's feather.

"The eagle is the most war-like bird," he began, "and the most kingly of all birds; besides, his feathers are unlike any others, and these are the reasons why they are used by our people to signify deeds of bravery.

"It is not true that when a man wears a feather bonnet, each one of the feathers represents the killing of a foe or even a *coup*. When a man wears an eagle feather upright upon his head, he is supposed to have counted one of four *coups* upon his enemy."

"Well, then, a *coup* does not mean the killing of an enemy?"

"No, it is the after-stroke or touching of the body after he falls. It is so ordered, because oftentimes the touching of an enemy is much more difficult to accomplish than the shooting of one from a distance. It requires a strong heart to face the whole body of the enemy, in order to count the *coup* on the fallen one, who lies under cover of his kinsmen's fire. Many a brave man has been lost in the attempt.

"When a warrior approaches his foe, dead or alive, he calls upon the other warriors to witness by saying: 'I, Fearless Bear, your brave, again perform the brave deed of counting the first (or second or third or fourth) *coup* upon the body of the bravest of your enemies.' Naturally, those who are present will see the act and be able to testify to it. When they return, the heralds, as you know, announce publicly all such deeds of valor, which then become a part of the man's war record. Any brave who would wear the eagle's feather must give proof of his right to do so.

"When a brave is wounded in the same battle where he counted his *coup*, he wears the feather hanging downward. When he is wounded, but makes no count, he trims his feather, and in that case it need not be an eagle feather. All other feathers are merely ornaments. When a warrior wears a feather with a round mark, it means that he slew his enemy. When the mark is cut into the feather and painted red, it means that he took the scalp.

"A brave who has been successful in ten battles is entitled to a war-bonnet; and if he is a recognized leader, he is permitted to wear one with long, trailing plumes. Also those who have counted many *coups* may tip the ends of the feathers with bits of white or colored down. Sometimes the eagle feather is tipped with a strip of weasel skin; that means the wearer had the honor of killing, scalping and counting the first *coup* upon the enemy all at the same time.

"This feather you have found was worn by a Cree—it is indiscriminately painted. All other feathers worn by the common Indians mean nothing," he added.

"Tell me, uncle, whether it would be proper for me to wear any feathers at all if I have never gone upon the war-path."

"You could wear any other kind of feathers, but not an eagle's," replied my uncle, "although sometimes one is worn on great occasions by the child of a noted man, to indicate the father's dignity and position."

The fire had gone down somewhat, so I pushed the embers together and wrapped my robe more closely about me. Now and then the ice on the lake would burst with a loud report like thunder. Uncheedah was busy re-stringing one of uncle's old snow-shoes. There were two different kinds that he wore; one with a straight toe and long; the other shorter and with an upturned toe. She had one of the shoes fastened toe down, between sticks driven into the ground, while she put in some new strings and tightened the others. Aunt Four Stars was beading a new pair of moccasins.

Wabeda, the dog, the companion of my boyhood days, was in trouble because he insisted upon bringing his extra bone into the teepee, while Uncheedah was determined that he should not. I sympathized with him, because I saw the matter as he did. If he should bury it in the snow outside, I knew Shunktokecha (the coyote) would surely steal it. I knew just how anxious Wabeda was about his bone. It was a fat bone—I mean a bone of a fat deer; and all Indians know how much better they are than the other kind.

Wabeda always hated to see a good thing go to waste. His eyes spoke words to me, for he and I had been friends for a long time. When I was afraid of anything in the woods, he would get in front of me at once and gently wag his tail. He always made it a point to look directly in my face. His kind, large eyes gave me a thousand assurances. When I was perplexed, he would hang about me until he understood the situation. Many times I believed he saved my life by uttering the dog word in time.

Most animals, even the dangerous grizzly, do not care to be seen when the two-legged kind and his dog are about. When I feared a surprise by a bear or a gray wolf, I would say to Wabeda: "Now, my dog, give your war-whoop!" and immediately he would sit up on his haunches and bark "to beat the band," as you white boys say. When a bear or wolf heard the noise, he would be apt to retreat.

Sometimes I helped Wabeda and gave a war-whoop of my own. This drove the deer away as well, but it relieved my mind.

When he appealed to me on this occasion, therefore, I said: "Come, my dog, let us bury your bone so that no Shunktokecha will take it."

He appeared satisfied with my suggestion, so we went out together.

We dug in the snow and buried our bone wrapped up in a piece of old blanket, partly burned; then we covered it up again with snow. We knew that the coyote would not touch anything burnt. I did not put it up a tree because Wabeda always objected to that, and I made it a point to consult his wishes whenever I could.

I came in and Wabeda followed me with two short rib bones in his mouth. Apparently he did not care to risk those delicacies.

"There," exclaimed Uncheedah, "you still insist upon bringing in some sort of bone!" but I begged her to let him gnaw them inside because it was so cold. Having been granted this privilege, he settled himself at my back and I became absorbed in some specially nice arrows that uncle was making.

"Oh, uncle, you must put on three feathers to all of them so that they can fly straight," I suggested.
"Yes, but if there are only two feathers, they will fly faster," he answered.
"Woow!" Wabeda uttered his suspicions.
"Woow!" he said again, and rushed for the entrance of the teepee. He kicked me over as he went and scattered the burning embers.
"En na he na!" Uncheedah exclaimed, but he was already outside.
"Wow, wow, wow! Wow, wow, wow!"
A deep guttural voice answered him. Out I rushed with my bow and arrows in my hand.
"Come, uncle, come! A big cinnamon bear!" I shouted as I emerged from the teepee.
Uncle sprang out, and in a moment he had sent a swift arrow through the bear's heart. The animal fell dead. He had just begun to dig up Wabeda's bone, when the dog's quick ear had heard the sound.
"Ah, uncle, Wabeda and I ought to have at least a little eaglet's feather for this! I too sent my small arrow into the bear before he fell," I exclaimed. "But I thought all bears ought to be in their lodges in the winter time. What was this one doing at this time of the year and night?"
"Well," said my uncle, "I will tell you. Among the tribes, some are naturally lazy. The cinnamon bear is the lazy one of his tribe. He alone sleeps out of doors in the winter, and because he has not a warm bed, he is soon hungry. Sometimes he lives in the hollow trunk of a tree, where he has made a bed of dry grass; but when the night is very cold, like to-night, he has to move about to keep himself from freezing, and as he prowls around, he gets hungry."
We dragged the huge carcass within our lodge. "Oh, what nice claws he has, uncle!" I exclaimed eagerly. "Can I have them for my necklace?"

"It is only the old medicine-men who wear them regularly. The son of a great warrior who has killed a grizzly may wear them upon a public occasion," he explained.
"And you are just like my father and are considered the best hunter among the Santees and Sissetons. You have killed many grizzlies, so that no one can object to my bear's-claw necklace," I said appealingly.
White Foot-print smiled. "My boy, you shall have them," he said, "but it is always better to earn them yourself." He cut the claws off carefully for my use.
"Tell me, uncle, whether you could wear these claws all the time?" I asked.
"Yes, I am entitled to wear them, but they are so heavy and uncomfortable," he replied, with a superior air.

At last the bear had been skinned and dressed and we all resumed our usual places. Uncheedah was particularly pleased to have some more fat for her cooking.

"Now, grandmother, tell me the story of the bear's fat. I shall be so happy if you will," I begged.

"It is a good story and it is true. You should know it by heart and gain a lesson from it," she replied. "It was in the forests of Minnesota, in the country that now belongs to the Ojibways. From the Bedawakanton Sioux village a young married couple went into the woods to get fresh venison. The snow was deep; the ice was thick. Far away in the woods they pitched their lonely teepee. The young man was a well-known hunter and his wife a good maiden of the village.

"He hunted entirely on snow-shoes, because the snow was very deep. His wife had to wear snow-shoes too, to get to the spot where they pitched their tent. It was thawing the day they went out, so their path was distinct after the freeze came again.

"The young man killed many deer and bears. His wife was very busy curing the meat and trying out the fat while he was away hunting each day. In the evenings she kept on trying the fat. He sat on one side of the teepee and she on the other.

"One evening, she had just lowered a kettle of fat to cool, and as she looked into the hot fat she saw the face of an Ojibway scout looking down at them through the smoke-hole. She said nothing, nor did she betray herself in any way.

"After a little she said to her husband in a natural voice: 'Marpeetopah, some one is looking at us through the smoke-hole, and I think it is an enemy's scout.'

"Then Marpeetopah (Four-skies) took up his bow and arrows and began to straighten and dry them for the next day's hunt, talking and laughing meanwhile. Suddenly he turned and sent an arrow upward, killing the Ojibway, who fell dead at their door.

"'Quick, Wadutah!' he exclaimed; 'you must hurry home upon our trail. I will stay here. When this scout does not return, the war-party may come in a body or send another scout. If only one comes, I can soon dispatch him and then I will follow you. If I do not do that, they will overtake us in our flight.'

"Wadutah (Scarlet) protested and begged to be allowed to stay with her husband, but at last she came away to get re-inforcements.

"Then Marpeetopah (Four-skies) put more sticks on the fire so that the teepee might be brightly lit and show him the way. He then took the scalp of the enemy and proceeded on his track, until he came to the upturned root of a great tree. There he spread out his arrows and laid out his tomahawk.

"Soon two more scouts were sent by the Ojibway war-party to see what was the trouble and why the first one failed to come back. He heard them as they approached. They were on snow-shoes. When they came close to him, he shot an arrow into the foremost. As for the other, in his effort to turn quickly his snow-shoes stuck in the deep snow and detained him, so Marpeetopah killed them both.

"Quickly he took the scalps and followed Wadutah. He ran hard. But the Ojibways suspected something wrong and came to the lonely teepee, to find all their scouts had been killed. They followed the path of Marpeetopah and Wadutah to the main village, and there a great battle was fought on the ice. Many were killed on both sides. It was after this that the Sioux moved to the Mississippi river."

I was sleepy by this time and I rolled myself up in my buffalo robe and fell asleep.

PART TWO
STORIES OF REAL INDIANS
I
WINONA'S CHILDHOOD

Hush, hushaby, little woman!
Be brave and weep not!
The spirits sleep not;
'Tis they who ordain
To woman, pain.
Hush, hushaby, little woman!
Now, all things bearing,
A new gift sharing
From those above—
To woman, love.
—*Sioux Lullaby.*

"Chinto, wéyanna! Yes, indeed; she is a real little woman," declares the old grandmother, as she receives and critically examines the tiny bit of humanity.

There is no remark as to the color of its hair or eyes, both so black as almost to be blue, but the old woman scans sharply the delicate profile of the baby face.

"Ah, she has the nose of her ancestors! Lips thin as a leaf, and eyes bright as stars in midwinter!" she exclaims, as she passes on the furry bundle to the other grandmother for her inspection.

"Tokee! she is pretty enough to win a twinkle from the evening star," remarks that smiling personage.

"And what shall her name be?

"Winona, the First-born, of course. That is hers by right of birth."

"Still, it may not fit her. One must prove herself worthy in order to retain that honorable name."

"Ugh," retorts the first grandmother, "she can at least bear it on probation!"

"Tosh, tosh," the other assents.

Thus the unconscious little Winona has passed the first stage of the Indian's christening.

Presently she is folded into a soft white doeskin, well lined with the loose down of cattails, and snugly laced into an upright oaken cradle, the front of which is a richly embroidered buckskin bag, with porcupine quills and deer's hoofs suspended from its profuse fringes. This gay cradle is strapped upon the second grandmother's back, and that dignitary walks off with the newcomer.

"You must come with me," she says. "We shall go among the father and mother trees, and hear them speak with their thousand tongues, that you may know their language forever. I will hang the cradle of the woman-child upon Utuhu, the oak; and she shall hear the love-sighs of the pine maiden!"

In this fashion Winona is introduced to nature and becomes at once "nature-born," in accord with the beliefs and practices of the wild red man.

The baby girl is called Winona for some months, when the medicine-man is summoned and requested to name publicly the first-born daughter of Chetonska, the White Hawk; but not until he has received a present of a good pony with a finely painted buffalo-robe. It is usual to confer another name besides that of the "First-born," which may be resumed later if the maiden proves worthy. The name Winona implies much of honor. It means charitable, kind, helpful; all that an eldest sister should be!

The herald goes around the ring of lodges announcing in singsong fashion the christening, and inviting everybody to a feast in honor of the event. A real American christening is always a gala occasion, when much savage wealth is distributed among the poor and old people. Winona has only just walked, and this fact is also announced with additional gifts. A well-born child is ever before the tribal eye and in the tribal ear, as every little step in its progress toward manhood or womanhood—the first time of walking or swimming, first shot with bow and arrow (if a boy), first pair of moccasins made (if a girl)—is announced publicly with feasting and the giving of presents.

So Winona receives her individual name of Tatiyopa, or Her Door. It is symbolic, like most Indian names, and implies that the door of the bearer is hospitable and her home attractive.

The two grandmothers, who have carried the little maiden upon their backs, now tell and sing to her by turns all the legends of their most noted female ancestors, from the twin sisters of the old story, the maidens who married among the star people of the sky, down to their own mothers. All their lullabies are feminine, and designed to impress upon her tender mind the life and duties of her sex.

As soon as she is old enough to play with dolls, she plays mother in all seriousness and gravity. She is dressed like a miniature woman (and her dolls are clad likewise), in garments of doeskin to her ankles, adorned with long fringes, embroidered with porcupine quills, and dyed with root dyes in various colors. Her little blanket or robe, with which she shyly drapes or screens her head and shoulders, is the skin of a buffalo calf or a deer, soft, white, embroidered on the smooth side, and often with the head and hoofs left on.

"You must never forget, my little daughter, that you are a woman like myself. Do always those things that you see me do," her mother often admonishes her.

Even the language of the Sioux has its feminine dialect, and the tiny girl would be greatly abashed were it ever needful to correct her for using a masculine termination.

This mother makes for her little daughter a miniature copy of every rude tool that she uses in her daily tasks. There is a little scraper of elk-horn to scrape raw-hides preparatory to tanning them, another scraper of a different shape for tanning, bone knives, and stone mallets for pounding choke-cherries and jerked meat.

While her mother is bending over a large buffalo-hide stretched and pinned upon the ground, standing upon it and scraping off the fleshy portion as nimbly as a carpenter shaves a board with his plane, Winona, at five years of age, stands upon a corner of the great hide and industriously scrapes away with her tiny instrument. When the mother stops to sharpen her tool, the little woman always sharpens hers also. Perhaps there is water to be fetched in bags made from the dried pericardium of an animal; the girl brings some in a smaller water-bag. When her mother goes for wood she carries one or two sticks on her back. She pitches her play teepee to form an exact copy of her mother's. Her little belongings are nearly all practical, and her very play is real!

II
WINONA'S GIRLHOOD

Braver than the bravest,
You sought honors at death's door;
Could you not remember
One who weeps at home—
Could you not remember me?
Braver than the bravest,
You sought honors more than love;
Dear, I weep, yet I am not a coward;
My heart weeps for thee—
My heart weeps when I remember thee!
—*Sioux Love Song.*

The sky is blue overhead, peeping through window-like openings in a roof of green leaves. Right between a great pine and a birch tree their soft doeskin shawls are spread, and there sit two Sioux maidens amid their fineries—variously colored porcupine quills for embroidery laid upon sheets of thin birch-bark, and moccasin tops worked in colors like autumn leaves. It is Winona and her friend Miniyata.

They have arrived at the period during which the young girl is carefully secluded from her brothers and cousins and future lovers, and retires, as it were, into the nunnery of the woods, behind a veil of thick foliage. Thus she is expected to develop her womanly qualities. In meditation and solitude, entirely alone or with a chosen companion of her own sex and age, she gains a secret strength, as she studies the art of womanhood from nature herself.

"Come, let us practise our sacred dance," says one to the other. Each crowns her glossy head with a wreath of wild flowers, and they dance with slow steps around the white birch, singing meanwhile the sacred songs.

Now upon the lake that stretches blue to the eastward there appears a distant canoe, a mere speck, no bigger than a bird far off against the shining sky.

"See the lifting of the paddles!" exclaims Winona.

"Like the leaping of a trout upon the water!" suggests Miniyata.

"I hope they will not discover us, yet I would like to know who they are," remarks the other, innocently.

The birch canoe approaches swiftly, with two young men plying the light cedar paddles.

The girls now settle down to their needle-work, quite as if they had never laughed or danced or woven garlands, bending over their embroidery in perfect silence. Surely they would not wish to attract attention, for the two sturdy young warriors have already landed.

They pick up the canoe and lay it well up on the bank, out of sight. Then one procures a strong pole. They lift a buck deer from the canoe—not a mark upon it, save for the bullet wound; the deer looks as if it were sleeping! They tie the hind legs together and the fore legs also and carry it between them on the pole.

Quickly and cleverly they do all this; and now they start forward and come unexpectedly upon the maidens' retreat! They pause for an instant in mute apology, but the girls smile their forgiveness, and the youths hurry on toward the village.

Winona has now attended her first maidens' feast and is considered eligible to marriage. She may receive young men, but not in public or in a social way, for such is not the custom of the Sioux. When he speaks, she need not answer him unless she chooses.

It was no disgrace to the chief's daughter in the old days to work with her hands. Indeed, their standard of worth was the willingness to work, but not for the sake of accumulation, only in order to give. Winona has learned to prepare skins, to remove the hair and tan the skin of a deer so that it may be made into moccasins within three days. She has a bone tool for each stage of the conversion of the stiff rawhide into velvety leather. She has been taught the art of painting tents and rawhide cases, and the manufacture of garments of all kinds.

Generosity is a trait that is highly developed in the Sioux woman. She makes many moccasins and other articles of clothing for her male relatives, or for any who are not well provided. She loves to see her brother the best dressed among the young men, and the moccasins especially of a young brave are the pride of his woman-kind.

Her own person is neatly attired, but ordinarily with great simplicity. Her doeskin gown has wide, flowing sleeves; the neck is low, but not so low as is the evening dress of society.

Her moccasins are plain; her leggins close-fitting and not as high as her brother's. She parts her smooth, jet-black hair in the middle and plaits it in two. In the old days she used to do it in one plait wound around with wampum. Her ornaments, sparingly worn, are beads, elks' teeth, and a touch of red paint. No feathers are worn by the woman, unless in a sacred dance. She is supposed to be always occupied with some feminine pursuit or engaged in some social affair, which also is strictly feminine as a rule.

There is an etiquette of sitting and standing, which is strictly observed. The woman must never raise her knees or cross her feet when seated. She seats herself on the ground sidewise, with both feet under her.

Notwithstanding her modesty and undemonstrative ways, there is no lack of mirth and relaxation for Winona among her girl companions.

In summer, swimming and playing in the water is a favorite amusement. She even imitates with the soles of her feet the peculiar, resonant sound that the beaver makes with her large, flat tail upon the surface of the water. She is a graceful swimmer, keeping the feet together and waving them backward and forward like the tail of a fish.

Nearly all her games are different from those of the men. She has a sport of wand-throwing, which develops fine muscles of the shoulder and back. The wands are about eight feet long, and taper gradually from an inch and a half to half an inch in diameter. Some of them are artistically made, with heads of bone and horn, so that it is remarkable to what a distance they may be made to slide over the ground. In the feminine game of ball, which is something like "shinny," the ball is driven with curved sticks between two goals. It is played with from two or three to a hundred on a side, and a game between two bands or villages is a picturesque event.

A common indoor diversion is the "deer's foot" game, played with six deer hoofs on a string, ending in a bone or steel awl. The object is to throw it in such a way as to catch one or more hoofs on the point of the awl, a feat which requires no little dexterity. Another is played with marked plum-stones in a bowl, which are thrown like dice and count according to the side that is turned uppermost.

Winona's wooing is a typical one. As with any other people, love-making is more or less in vogue at all times of the year, but more especially at midsummer, during the characteristic reunions and festivities of that season. The young men go about usually in pairs, and the maidens do likewise. They may meet by chance at any time of day, in the woods or at the spring, but oftenest seek to do so after dark, just outside the teepee. The girl has her companion, and he has his, for the sake of propriety or protection. The conversation is carried on in a whisper, so that even these chaperons do not hear.

At the sound of the drum on summer evenings, dances are begun within the circular rows of teepees, but without the circle the young men promenade in pairs. Each provides himself with the plaintive flute and plays the simple cadences of his people, while his person is completely covered with his fine robe, so that he cannot be recognized by the passer-by. At every pause in the melody he gives his yodel-like love-call, to which the girls respond with their musical, sing-song laughter.

Matosapa has improved every opportunity, until Winona has at last shyly admitted her willingness to listen. For a whole year he has been compelled at intervals to repeat the story of his love. Through the autumn hunting of the buffalo and the long, cold winter he often presents her kinsfolk with his game.

At the next midsummer the parents on both sides are made acquainted with the betrothal, and they at once begin preparations for the coming wedding. Provisions and delicacies of all kinds are laid aside for a feast. Matosapa's sisters and his girl cousins are told of the approaching event, and they too prepare for it, since it is their duty to dress or adorn the bride with garments made by their own hands.

The bride is ceremoniously delivered to her husband's people, together with presents of rich clothing, collected from all her clan, which she afterward distributes among her new relations. Winona is carried in a travois handsomely decorated, and is received with equal ceremony.

III
A MIDSUMMER FEAST

The Wahpetonwan village on the banks of the Minnesota river was alive with the newly-arrived guests and the preparations for the coming event. Meat of wild game had been put away with much care during the previous fall in anticipation of this feast. There was wild rice and the choicest of dried venison that had been kept all winter, as well as freshly dug turnips, ripe berries and an abundance of fresh meat.

Along the edge of the woods the teepees were pitched in groups or semi-circles, each band distinct from the others. The teepee of Mankato or Blue Earth was pitched in a conspicuous spot. Just over the entrance was painted in red and yellow a picture of a pipe, and directly opposite this the rising sun. The painting was symbolic of welcome and good will to men under the bright sun.

A meeting was held to appoint some "medicine-man" to make the balls that were to be used in the lacrosse contest; and presently the herald announced that this honor had been conferred upon old Chankpee-yuhah, or "Keeps the Club," while every other man of his profession was disappointed.

Towards evening he appeared in the circle, leading by the hand a boy about four years old. Closely the little fellow observed every motion of the man; nothing escaped his vigilant black eyes, which seemed constantly to grow brighter and larger, while his glossy black hair was plaited and wound around his head like that of a Celestial. He wore a bit of swan's down in each ear, which formed a striking contrast with the child's complexion. Further than this, the boy was painted according to the fashion of the age. He held in his hands a miniature bow and arrows.

The medicine-man drew himself up in an admirable attitude, and proceeded to make his short speech:

"Wahpetonwans, you boast that you run down the elk; you can outrun the Ojibways. Before you all, I dedicate to you this red ball. Kaposias, you claim that no one has a lighter foot than you; you declare that you can endure running a whole day without water. To you I dedicate this black ball. Either you or the Leaf-Dwellers will have to drop your eyes and bow your head when the game is over. I wish to announce that if the Wahpetonwans should win, this little warrior shall bear the name Ohiyesa (winner) through life; but if the Light Lodges should win, let the name be given to any child appointed by them."

The ground selected for the great game was on a narrow strip of land between a lake and the river. It was about three quarters of a mile long and a quarter of a mile in width. The spectators had already ranged themselves all along the two sides, as well as at the two ends, which were somewhat higher than the middle. The soldiers appointed to keep order furnished much of the entertainment of the day. They painted artistically and tastefully, according to the Indian fashion, not only their bodies but also their ponies and clubs. They were so strict in enforcing the laws that no one could venture with safety within a few feet of the limits of the field.

Now all of the minor events and feasts, occupying several days' time, had been observed. Heralds on ponies' backs announced that all who intended to participate in the final game were requested to repair to the ground; also that if any one bore a grudge against another, he was implored to forget his ill-feeling until the contest should be over.

The most powerful men were stationed at the half-way ground, while the fast runners were assigned to the back. It was an impressive spectacle a fine collection of agile forms, almost stripped of garments and painted in wild imitation of the rainbow and sunset sky on human canvas. Some had undertaken to depict the Milky Way across their tawny bodies, and one or two made a bold attempt to reproduce the lightning. Others contented themselves with painting the figure of some fleet animal or swift bird on their muscular chests.

At the middle of the ground were stationed four immense men, magnificently formed. A fifth approached this group, paused a moment, and then threw his head back, gazed up into the sky in the manner of a cock and gave a smooth, clear operatic tone. Instantly the little black ball went up between the two middle rushers, in the midst of yells, cheers and war-whoops. Both men endeavored to catch it in the air; but alas! each interfered with the other; then the guards on each side rushed upon them. For a time, a hundred lacrosse sticks vied with each other, and the wriggling human flesh and paint were all one could see through the cloud of dust. Suddenly there shot swiftly through the air toward the south, toward the Kaposias' goal, the ball. There was a general cheer from their adherents, which echoed back from the white cliff on the opposite side of the Minnesota.

As the ball flew through the air, two adversaries were ready to receive it. The Kaposia quickly met the ball, but failed to catch it in his netted bag, for the other had swung his up like a flash. Thus it struck the ground, but had no opportunity to bound up when a Wahpeton pounced upon it like a cat and slipped out of the grasp of his opponents. A mighty cheer thundered through the air.

The warrior who had undertaken to pilot the little sphere was risking much, for he must dodge a host of Kaposias before he could gain any ground. He was alert and agile; now springing like a panther, now leaping like a deer over a stooping opponent who tried to seize him around the waist. Every opposing player was upon his heels, while those of his own side did all in their power to clear the way for him. But it was all in vain. He only gained fifty paces.

Thus the game went. First one side, then the other would gain an advantage, and then it was lost, until the herald proclaimed that it was time to change the ball. No victory was in sight for either side.

After a few minutes' rest, the game was resumed. The red ball was now tossed in the air in the usual way. No sooner had it descended than one of the rushers caught it and away it went northward; again it was fortunate, for it was advanced by one of the same side. The scene was now one of the wildest excitement and confusion. At last, the northward flight of the ball was checked for a moment and a desperate struggle ensued.

The ball had not been allowed to come to the surface since it reached this point, for there were more than a hundred men who scrambled for it. Suddenly a warrior shot out of the throng like the ball itself! Then some of the players shouted: "Look out for Antelope!" But it was too late. The little sphere had already nestled into Antelope's palm and that fleetest of Wahpetons had thrown down his lacrosse stick and set a determined eye upon the northern goal.

Such a speed! He had cleared almost all the opponents' guards—there were but two more. These were exceptional runners of the Kaposias. As he approached them in his almost irresistible speed, every savage heart thumped louder in the Indian's dusky bosom. In another moment there would be a defeat for the Kaposias or a prolongation of the game. The two men, with a determined look approached their foe like two panthers prepared to spring; yet he neither slackened his speed nor deviated from his course. A crash—a mighty shout!—the two Kaposias collided, and the swift Antelope had won the laurels!

The turmoil and commotion at the victors' camp were indescribable. A few beats of a drum were heard, after which the criers hurried along the lines, announcing the last act to be performed at the camp of the "Leaf Dwellers."

The day had been a perfect one. Every event had been a success; and, as a matter of course, the old people were happy, for they largely profited by these occasions. Within the circle formed by the general assembly sat in a group the members of the common council. Blue Earth arose, and in a few appropriate and courteous remarks assured his guests that it was not selfishness that led his braves to carry off the honors of the last event, but that this was a friendly contest in which each band must assert its prowess. In memory of this victory, the boy would now receive his name. A loud "Ho-o-o" of approbation reverberated from the edge of the forest upon the Minnesota's bank.

Half frightened, the little fellow was now brought into the circle, looking very much as if he were about to be executed. Cheer after cheer went up for the awe-stricken boy. Chankpee-yuhah, the medicine-man, proceeded to confer the name.

"Ohiyesa (or Winner) shall be thy name henceforth. Be brave, be patient and thou shalt always win! Thy name is Ohiyesa."

IV
THE FAITHFULNESS OF LONG EARS

Away beyond the Thin Hills, above the Big Lone Tree upon the Powder river, the Uncpapa Sioux had celebrated their Sun Dance, some forty years ago. It was midsummer and the red folk were happy. They lacked for nothing. The yellowish green flat on either side of the Powder was studded with wild flowers, and the cottonwood trees were in full leaf. One large circle of buffalo-skin teepees formed the movable village.

The tribal rites had all been observed, and the usual summer festivities enjoyed to the full. The camp as it broke up divided itself in three parts, each of which had determined to seek a favorite hunting-ground.

One band journeyed west, toward the Tongue river. One followed a tributary of the Powder to the south. The third merely changed camp, on account of the grazing for ponies, and for four days remained near the old place.

The party that went west did not fail to realize the perilous nature of their wanderings, for they were trespassing upon the country of the warlike Crows.

On the third day at sunrise, the Sioux crier's voice resounded in the valley of the Powder, announcing that the lodges must be razed and the villagers must take up their march.

Breakfast of jerked buffalo meat had been served and the women were adjusting their packs, not without much chatter and apparent confusion. Weeko (Beautiful Woman), the young wife of the war-chief Shunkaska, who had made many presents at the dances in honor of her twin boys, now gave one of her remaining ponies to a poor old woman whose only beast of burden, a large dog, had died during the night.

This made it necessary to shift the packs of the others. Nakpa, or Long Ears, her kitten-like gray mule, which had heretofore been honored with the precious burden of the twin babies, was to be given a heavier and more cumbersome load. Weeko's two-year-old spotted pony was selected to carry the babies.

Accordingly, the two children, in their gorgeously beaded buckskin hoods, were suspended upon either side of the pony's saddle. As Weeko's first-born, they were beautifully dressed; even the saddle and bridle were daintily worked by her own hands.

The caravan was now in motion, and Weeko started all her ponies after the leader, while she adjusted the mule's clumsy burden of kettles and other household gear. In a moment:

"Go on, let us see how you move with your new load! Go on!" she exclaimed again, with a light blow of the horse-hair lariat, as the animal stood perfectly still.

Nakpa simply gave an angry side glance at her load and shifted her position once or twice. Then she threw herself headlong into the air and landed stiff-legged, uttering at the same time her unearthly protest. First she dove straight through the crowd, then proceeded in a circle, her heels describing wonderful curves and sweeps in the air. Her pack, too, began to come to pieces and to take forced flights from her undignified body and heels, in the midst of the screams of women and children, the barking of dogs, and the war-whoops of the amused young braves.

The cowskin tent became detached from her saddle, and a moment later Nakpa stood free. Her sides worked like a bellows as she stood there, meekly indignant, apparently considering herself to be the victim of an uncalled-for misunderstanding.

"I should put an arrow through her at once, only she is not worth a good arrow," said Shunkaska, or White Dog, the husband of Weeko. At his wife's answer, he opened his eyes in surprised displeasure.

"No, she shall have her own pack again. She wants her twins. I ought never to have taken them from her!"

Weeko approached Nakpa as she stood alone and unfriended in the face of her little world, all of whom considered that she had committed the unpardonable sin. As for her, she evidently felt that her misfortunes had not been of her own making. She gave a hesitating, sidelong look at her mistress.

"Nakpa, you should not have acted so. I knew you were stronger than the others, therefore I gave you that load," said Weeko in a conciliatory tone, and patted her on the nose. "Come, now, you shall have your own pet pack," and she led her back to where the young pony stood silently with the babies.

Nakpa threw back her ears and cast savage looks at him, while Shunkaska, with no small annoyance, gathered together as much as he could of their scattered household effects. The sleeping brown-skinned babies in their chrysalis-like hoods were gently lowered from the pony's back and attached securely to Nakpa's padded wooden saddle. The family pots and kettles were divided among the pack-ponies. Order was restored and the village once more in motion.

"Come now, Nakpa; you have your wish. You must take good care of my babies. Be good, because I have trusted you," murmured the young mother in her softest tones.

"Really, Weeko, you have some common ground with Nakpa, for you both always want to have your own way, and stick to it, too! I tell you, I fear this Long Ears. She is not to be trusted with babies," remarked Shunkaska, with a good deal of severity.

But his wife made no reply, for she well knew that though he might criticize, he would not actually interfere with her domestic arrangements. He now started ahead to join the men in advance of the slow-moving procession, thus leaving her in undivided charge of her household. One or two of the pack ponies were not well trained and required all her attention. Nakpa had been a faithful servant until her escapade of the morning, and she was now obviously satisfied with her mistress' arrangements. She walked alongside with her lariat dragging, and perfectly free to do as she pleased.

Some hours later, the party ascended a slope from the river bottom to cross over the divide which lay between the Powder River and a tributary stream. The ford was deep, with a swift current. Here and there a bald butte stood out in full relief against the brilliant blue sky.

"Whoo! whoo!" came the blood-curdling signal of danger from the front. It was no unfamiliar sound—the rovers knew it only too well. It meant sudden death—or at best a cruel struggle and frantic flight.

Terrified, yet self-possessed, the women turned to fly while yet there was time. Instantly the mother looked to Nakpa, who carried on either side of the saddle her precious boys. She hurriedly examined the fastenings to see that all was secure, and then caught her swiftest pony, for, like all Indian women, she knew just what was happening, and that while her husband was engaged in front with the enemy, she must seek safety with her babies.

Hardly was she in the saddle when a heartrending war-whoop sounded on their flank, and she knew that they were surrounded! Instinctively she reached for her husband's second quiver of arrows, which was carried by one of the pack-ponies. Alas! the Crow warriors were already upon them! The ponies became unmanageable, and the wild screams of women and children pierced the awful confusion.

Quick as a flash, Weeko turned again to her babies, but Nakpa had already disappeared!

When the Crows made their flank charge, Nakpa apparently appreciated the situation. To save herself and the babies, she took a desperate chance. She fled straight through the attacking force.

When the warriors came howling upon her in great numbers, she at once started back the way she had come, to the camp left behind. They had travelled nearly three days. To be sure, they did not travel more than fifteen miles a day, but it was full forty miles to cover before dark.

"Look! look!" exclaimed a warrior, "two babies hung from the saddle of a mule!"

No one heeded this man's call, and his arrow did not touch Nakpa or either of the boys, but it struck the thick part of the saddle over the mule's back.

"Whoo! whoo!" yelled another Crow to his comrades, "the Sioux have dispatched a runner to get reinforcements! There he goes, down on the flat! Now he has almost reached the river bottom!"

It was only Nakpa. She laid back her ears and stretched out more and more to gain the river, for she realized that when she had crossed the ford the Crows would not pursue her farther.

Now she had reached the bank. With the intense heat from her exertions, she was extremely nervous, and she imagined a warrior behind every bush. Yet she had enough sense left to realize that she must not satisfy her thirst. She tried the bottom with her forefoot, then waded carefully into the deep stream.

She kept her big ears well to the front as she swam, to catch the slightest sound. As she stepped on the opposite shore, she shook herself and the boys vigorously, then pulled a few mouthfuls of grass and started on.

Soon one of the babies began to cry, and the other was not long in joining him. Nakpa did not know what to do. She gave a gentle whinny and both babies apparently stopped to listen; then she took up an easy gait as if to put them to sleep.

These tactics answered only for a time. As she fairly flew over the lowlands, the babies' hunger increased and they screamed so loud that a passing coyote had to sit upon his haunches and wonder what in the world the fleeing long-eared horse was carrying on his saddle. Even magpies and crows flew near as if to ascertain the meaning of this curious sound.

Nakpa now came to the Little Trail creek, a tributary of the Powder, not far from the old camp. There she swerved aside so suddenly as almost to jerk her babies out of their cradles. Two gray wolves, one on each side, approached her, growling low—their white teeth showing.

Never in her humble life had Nakpa been in more desperate straits. The larger of the wolves came fiercely forward to engage her attention, while his mate was to attack her behind and cut her hamstrings. But for once the pair had made a miscalculation. The mule used her front hoofs vigorously on the foremost wolf, while her hind ones were doing even more effective work. The larger wolf soon went limping away with a broken hip, and the one in the rear received a deep cut on the jaw which proved an effectual discouragement.

A little further on, an Indian hunter drew near on horseback, but Nakpa did not pause or slacken her pace. On she fled through the long dry grass of the river bottoms, while her babies slept again from sheer exhaustion. Toward sunset, she entered the Sioux camp amid great excitement, for some one had spied her afar off, and the boys and the dogs announced her coming.

"Whoo, whoo! Weeko's Nakpa has come back with the twins! Whoo, whoo!" exclaimed the men. "Tokee! tokec!" cried the women.

Zeezeewin, a sister to Weeko, who was in the village, came forward and released the children, as Nakpa gave a low whinny and stopped.

"Sing a Brave-Heart song for the Long-Eared One! She has escaped alone with her charge. She is entitled to wear an eagle's feather! Look at the arrow in her saddle! and more, she has a knife-wound in her jaw and an arrow-cut on her hind leg.—No, those are the marks of a wolf's teeth! She has passed through many dangers and saved two chief's sons, who will some day make the Crows sorry for this day's work!"

The speaker was an old man, who thus addressed the fast gathering throng.

Zeezeewin now came forward again with an eagle feather and some white paint in her hands. The young men rubbed Nakpa down, and the feather, marked with red to indicate her wounds, was fastened to her mane. Shoulders and hips were touched with red paint to show her endurance in running. Then the crier, praising her brave deed in heroic verse, led her around the camp, inside of the circle of teepees. All the people stood outside their lodges and listened respectfully, for the Dakota loves well to honor the faithful and the brave.

During the next day, riders came in from the ill-fated party, bringing the sad news of the fight and heavy loss. Late in the afternoon came Weeko, her face swollen with crying, her beautiful hair cut short in mourning, her garments torn and covered with dust and blood. Her husband had fallen in the fight, and her twin boys she supposed to have been taken captive by the Crows. Singing in a hoarse voice the praises of her departed warrior, she entered the camp. As she approached her sister's teepee, there stood Nakpa, still wearing her honorable decorations. At the same moment, Zeezeewin came out to meet her with both babies in her arms.

"Mechinkshee! mechinkshee! (my sons, my sons!)" was all that the poor mother could say, as she all but fell from the saddle to the ground. The despised Long Ears had not betrayed her trust.

V
SNANA'S FAWN
The Little Missouri was in her spring fulness, and the hills among which she found her way to the Great Muddy were profusely adorned with colors, much like those worn by the wild red man upon a holiday! Between the gorgeous buttes and rainbow-tinted ridges there were narrow plains, broken here and there by dry creeks or gulches, and these again were clothed scantily with poplars and sad-colored bull-berry bushes, while the bare spots were purple with the wild Dakota crocuses.

Upon the lowest of a series of natural terraces there stood on this May morning a young Sioux girl, whose graceful movements were not unlike those of a doe which chanced to be lurking in a neighboring gulch. On the upper plains, not far away, were her young companions, all busily employed with the wewoptay, as it is called—the sharp-pointed stick with which the Sioux women dig wild turnips. They were gayly gossiping together, or each humming a love-song as she worked, only Snana stood somewhat apart from the rest; in fact, concealed by the crest of the ridge.

It was now full-born day. The sun shone hot upon the bare ground, and the drops stood upon Snana's forehead as she plied her long pole. There was a cool spring in the dry creek bed near by, well hidden by a clump of choke-cherry bushes, and she turned thither to cool her thirsty throat. In the depths of the ravine her eye caught a familiar footprint—the track of a doe with the young fawn beside it. The hunting instinct arose within.

"It will be a great feat if I can find and take from her the babe. The little tawny skin shall be beautifully dressed by my mother. The legs and the nose shall be embossed with porcupine quills. It will be my work-bag," she said to herself.

As she stole forward on the fresh trail she scanned every nook, every clump of bushes. There was a sudden rustle from within a grove of wild plum trees, thickly festooned with grape and clematis, and the doe mother bounded away as carelessly as if she were never to return.

Ah, a mother's ruse! Snana entered the thorny enclosure, which was almost a rude teepee, and, tucked away in the further-most corner, lay something with a trout-like, speckled, tawny coat. She bent over it. The fawn was apparently sleeping. Presently its eyes moved a bit, and a shiver passed through its subtle body.

"Thou shalt not die; thy skin shall not become my work-bag!" unconsciously the maiden spoke. The mother sympathy had taken hold on her mind. She picked the fawn up tenderly, bound its legs, and put it on her back to carry like an Indian babe in the folds of her robe.

"I cannot leave you alone, Tachinchala. Your mother is not here. Our hunters will soon return by this road, and your mother has left behind her two plain tracks leading to this thicket," she murmured.

The wild creature struggled vigorously for a minute, and then became quiet. Its graceful head protruded from the elk-skin robe just over Snana's shoulder. She was slowly climbing the slope with her burden, when suddenly like an apparition the doe mother stood before her. The fawn called loudly when it was first seized, and the mother was not too far away to hear. Now she called frantically for her child, at the same time stamping with her delicate forefeet.

"Yes, sister, you are right; she is yours; but you cannot save her to-day! The hunters will soon be here. Let me keep her for you; I will return her to you safely. And hear me, O sister of the woods, that some day I may become the mother of a noble race of warriors and of fine women, as handsome as you are!"

At this moment the quick eyes of the Indian girl detected something strange in the doe's actions. She glanced in every direction and behold! a grizzly bear was cautiously approaching the group from a considerable distance.

"Run, run, sister! I shall save your child if I can," she cried, and flew for the nearest scrub oak on the edge of the bank. Up the tree she scrambled, with the fawn still securely bound to her back. The grizzly came on with teeth exposed, and the doe-mother in her flight came between him and the tree, giving a series of indignant snorts as she ran, and so distracted Mato from his object of attack; but only for a few seconds—then on he came!

"Desist, O brave Mato! It does not become a great medicine-man to attack a helpless woman with a burden upon her back!"

Snana spoke as if the huge brute could understand her, and, indeed, the Indians hold that wild animals understand intuitively when appealed to by human beings in distress. Yet he replied only with a hoarse growl, as rising upon his hind legs he shook the little tree vigorously.

"Ye, ye, heyupi ye!" Snana called loudly to her companion turnip-diggers. Her cry soon brought all the women into sight upon a near-by ridge, and they immediately gave a general alarm. Mato saw them, but appeared not at all concerned and was still intent upon dislodging the girl, who clung frantically to her perch.

Presently there appeared upon the little knoll several warriors, mounted and uttering the usual war-whoop, as if they were about to swoop down upon a human enemy. This touched the dignity of Mato, and he immediately prepared to accept the challenge. Every Indian was alive to the possibilities of the occasion, for it is well known that Mato, or grizzly bear, alone among animals is given the rank of a warrior, so that whoever conquers him may wear an eagle feather.

"Woo! woo!" the warriors shouted, as they maneuvered to draw him into the open plain.

He answered with hoarse growls, threatening a rider who had ventured too near. But arrows were many and well-aimed, and in a few minutes the great and warlike Mato lay dead at the foot of the tree.

The men ran forward and counted their *coups* on him, just as when an enemy is fallen. Then they looked at one another and placed their hands over their mouths as the young girl descended the-tree with a fawn bound upon her back.

"So that was the bait!" they cried. "And will you not make a feast with that fawn for us who came to your rescue?"

"The fawn is young and tender, and we have not eaten meat for two days. It will be a generous thing to do," added her father, who was among them.

"Ye-e-e!" she cried out in distress. "Do not ask it! I have seen this fawn's mother. I have promised to keep her child safe. See! I have saved its life, even when my own was in danger."

"Ho, ho, wakan ye lo! (Yes, yes, 'tis holy or mysterious)," they exclaimed approvingly.

It was no small trouble for Snana to keep her trust. As may well be supposed, all the dogs of the teepee village must be watched and kept at a distance. Neither was it easy to feed the little captive; but in gaining its confidence the girl was an adept. The fawn soon followed her everywhere, and called to her when hungry exactly as she had called to her own mother.

After several days, when her fright at the encounter with the bear had somewhat worn off, Snana took her pet into the woods and back to the very spot in which she had found it. In the furthest corner of the wild plum grove she laid it down, gently stroked its soft forehead, and smoothed the leaf-like ears. The little thing closed its eyes. Once more the Sioux girl bent over and laid her cheek against the fawn's head; then reluctantly she moved away, hoping and yet dreading that the mother would return. She crouched under a clump of bushes near by, and gave the doe call. It was a reckless thing for her to do, for such a call might bring upon her a mountain lion or ever-watchful silver-tip; but Snana did not think of that.

In a few minutes she heard the light patter of hoofs, and caught a glimpse of a doe running straight toward the fawn's hiding-place. When she stole near enough to see, the doe and the fawn were examining one another carefully, as if fearing some treachery. At last both were apparently satisfied. The doe caressed her natural child, and the little one accepted the milk she offered.

In the Sioux maiden's mind there was turmoil. A close attachment to the little wild creature had already taken root there, contending with the sense of justice that was strong within her. Now womanly sympathy for the mother was in control, and now a desire to possess and protect her helpless pet.

"I can take care of her against all hunters, both animal and human. They are ever ready to seize the helpless fawn for food. Her life will be often exposed. You cannot save her from disaster. O, Takcha, my sister, let me still keep her for you!" she finally appealed to the poor doe, who was nervously watching the intruder, and apparently thinking how she might best escape with the fawn.

Just at this moment there came a low call from the wood. It was a doe call; but the wild mother and her new friend both knew that it was not the call of a real doe.

"It is a Sioux hunter!" whispered the girl. "You must go, my sister! Be off; I will take your child to safety!"

While she was yet speaking, the doe seemed to realize the danger. She stopped only an instant to lick fondly the tawny coat of the little one, then she bounded away.

As Snana emerged from the bushes with her charge, a young hunter met her face to face, and stared at her curiously. He was not of her father's camp, but a stranger.

"Ugh, you have my game."

"Tosh!" she replied coquettishly.

It was so often said among the Indians that the doe was wont to put on human form to mislead the hunter, that it looked strange to see a woman with a fawn, and the young man could not forbear to gaze upon Snana.

"You are not the real mother in maiden's guise? Tell me truly if you are of human blood," he demanded rudely.

"I am a Sioux maiden! Do you not know my father?" she replied.
"Ah, but who is your father? What is his name?" he insisted, nervously fingering his arrows.
"Do not be a coward! Surely you should know a maid of your own race," she replied reproachfully.
"Ah, you know the tricks of the doe! What is thy name?"
"Hast thou forgotten the etiquette of thy people, and wouldst compel me to pronounce my own name? I refuse; thou art jesting!" she retorted with a smile.
"Thou dost give the tricky answers of a doe. I cannot wait; I must act before I lose my natural mind. But already I am yours. Whatever purpose you may have in thus charming a poor hunter, be merciful," and, throwing aside his quiver, he sat down.
The maiden stole a glance at his face and then another. He was handsome. Softly she reëntered the thicket and laid down the little fawn.
"Promise me never to hunt here again!" she said earnestly, as she came forth without her pretty burden, and he exacted another promise in return. Thus Snana lost her fawn, and found a lover.

VI
HAKADAH'S FIRST OFFERING

"Hakadah, coowah!" was the sonorous call that came from a large teepee in the midst of the Indian encampment. In answer to the summons there emerged from the woods, which were only a few steps away, a boy, accompanied by a splendid black dog. There was little in the appearance of the little fellow to distinguish him from the other Sioux boys.

He hastened to the tent from which he had been summoned, carrying in his hands a bow and arrows gorgeously painted, while the small birds and squirrels that he had killed with these weapons dangled from his belt. Within the tent sat two old women, one on each side of the fire. Uncheedah was the boy's grandmother, who had brought up the motherless child. Wahchewin was only a caller, but she had been invited to remain and assist in the first personal offering of Hakadah to the "Great Mystery."

It had been whispered through the teepee village that Uncheedah intended to give a feast in honor of her grandchild's first sacrificial offering. This was mere speculation, however, for the clear-sighted old woman had determined to keep this part of the matter secret until the offering should be completed, believing that the "Great Mystery" should be met in silence and dignity.

The boy came rushing into the lodge, followed by his dog Ohitika, who was wagging his tail promiscuously, as if to say: "Master and I are really hunters!"

Hakadah breathlessly gave a descriptive narrative of the killing of each bird and squirrel as he pulled them off his belt and threw them before his grandmother.

"This blunt-headed arrow," said he, "actually had eyes this morning. Before the squirrel can dodge around the tree it strikes him in the head, and, as he falls to the ground, my Ohitika is upon him."

He knelt upon one knee as he talked, his black eyes shining like evening stars.

"Sit down here," said Uncheedah to the boy; "I have something to say to you. You see that you are now almost a man. Observe the game you have brought me! It will not be long before you will leave me, for a warrior must seek opportunities to make him great among his people.

"You must endeavor to equal your father and grandfather," she went on. "They were warriors and feast-makers. But it is not the poor hunter who makes many feasts. Do you not remember the 'Legend of the Feast-Maker,' who gave forty feasts in twelve moons? And have you forgotten the story of the warrior who sought the will of the Great Mystery? To-day you will make your first offering to him."

The concluding sentence fairly dilated the eyes of the young hunter, for he felt that a great event was about to occur, in which he would be the principal actor. But Uncheedah resumed her speech.

"You must give up one of your belongings—whichever is dearest to you—for this is to be a sacrificial offering."

This somewhat confused the boy; not that he was selfish, but rather uncertain as to what would be the most appropriate thing to give. Then, too, he supposed that his grandmother referred to his ornaments and playthings only. So he volunteered:

"I can give up my best bow and arrows, and all the paints I have, and—and my bear's claws necklace, grandmother!"

"Are these the things dearest to you?" she demanded.

"Not the bow and arrows, but the paints will be very hard to get, for there are no white people near; and the necklace—it is not easy to get one like it again. I will also give up my otter-skin head-dress, if you think that it not enough."

"But think, my boy, you have not yet mentioned the thing that will be a pleasant offering to the Great Mystery."

The boy looked into the woman's face with a puzzled expression.

"I have nothing else as good as those things I have named, grandmother, unless it is my spotted pony; and I am sure that the Great Mystery will not require a little boy to make him so large a gift. Besides, my uncle gave three otter-skins and five eagle-feathers for him and I promised to

keep him a long while, if the Blackfeet or the Crows do not steal him."
Uncheedah was not fully satisfied with the boy's free offerings. Perhaps it had not occurred to him what she really wanted. But Uncheedah knew where his affection was vested. His faithful dog, his pet and companion—Hakadah was almost inseparable from the loving beast.
She was sure that it would be difficult to obtain his consent to sacrifice the animal, but she ventured upon a final appeal.
"You must remember," she said, "that in this offering you will call upon him who looks at you from every creation. In the wind you hear him whisper to you. He gives his war-whoop in the thunder. He watches you by day with his eye, the sun; at night, he gazes upon your sleeping countenance through the moon. In short, it is the Mystery of Mysteries, who controls all things, to whom you will make your first offering. By this act, you will ask him to grant to you what he has granted to few men. I know you wish to be a great warrior and hunter. I am not prepared to see my Hakadah show any cowardice, for the love of possessions is a woman's trait and not a brave's."
During this speech, the boy had been completely aroused to the spirit of manliness, and in his excitement was willing to give up anything he had—even his pony! But he was unmindful of his friend and companion, Ohitika, the dog! So, scarcely had Uncheedah finished speaking, when he almost shouted:
"Grandmother, I will give up any of my possessions for the offering to the Great Mystery! You may select what you think will be most pleasing to him."
There were two silent spectators of this little dialogue. One was Wahchewin, the other was Ohitika. The woman had been invited to stay, although only a neighbor. The dog, by force of habit, had taken up his usual position by the side of his master when they entered the teepee. Without moving a muscle, save those of his eyes, he had been a very close observer of what passed.
Had the dog but moved once to attract the attention of his little friend, he might have been dissuaded from that impetuous exclamation: "Grandmother, I will give up any of my possessions!"
It was hard for Uncheedah to tell the boy that he must part with his dog, but she was equal to the situation.
"Hakadah," she proceeded cautiously, "you are a young brave. I know, though young, your heart is strong and your courage is great. You will be pleased to give up the dearest thing you have for your first offering. You must give up Ohitika. He is brave; and you, too, are brave. He will not fear death; you will bear his loss bravely. Come,—here are four bundles of paints and a filled pipe,—let us go to the place!"

When the last words were uttered, Hakadah did not seem to hear them. He was simply unable to speak. To a civilized eye, he would have appeared at that moment like a little copper statue. His bright black eyes were fast melting in floods of tears, when he caught his grandmother's eye and recollected her oft-repeated adage: "Tears for woman and the war-whoop for man to drown sorrow!"

He swallowed two or three big mouthfuls of heartache and the little warrior was master of the situation.

"Grandmother, my Brave will have to die! Let me tie together two of the prettiest tails of the squirrels that he and I killed this morning, to show to the Great Mystery what a hunter he has been. Let me paint him myself."

This request Uncheedah could not refuse, and she left the pair alone for a few minutes, while she went to ask Wacoota to execute Ohitika.

Every Indian boy knows that, when a warrior is about to meet death, he must sing a death dirge. Hakadah thought of his Ohitika as a person who would meet his death without a struggle, so he began to sing a dirge for him, at the same time hugging him tight to himself. As if he were a human being, he whispered in his ear:

"Be brave, my Ohitika! I shall remember you the first time I am upon the war-path in the Ojibway country."

At last he heard Uncheedah talking with a man outside the teepee, so he quickly took up his paints. Ohitika was a jet-black dog, with a silver tip on the end of his tail and on his nose, beside one white paw and a white star upon a protuberance between his ears. Hakadah knew that a man who prepares for death usually paints with red and black. Nature had partially provided Ohitika in this respect, so that only red was required and this Hakadah supplied generously.

Then he took off a piece of red cloth and tied it around the dog's neck; to this he fastened two of the squirrels' tails and a wing from the oriole they had killed that morning.

Just then it occurred to him that good warriors always mourn for their departed friends, and the usual mourning was black paint. He loosened his black braided locks, ground a dead coal, mixed it with bear's oil and rubbed it on his entire face.

During this time every hole in the tent was occupied with an eye. Among the lookers-on was his grandmother. She was very near relenting. Had she not feared the wrath of the Great Mystery, she would have been happy to call out to the boy: "Keep your dear dog, my child!"

As it was, Hakadah came out of the teepee with his face looking like an eclipsed moon, leading his beautiful dog, who was even handsomer than ever with the red touches on his specks of white.

It was now Uncheedah's turn to struggle with the storm and burden in her soul. But the boy was emboldened by the people's admiration of his bravery, and did not shed a tear. As soon as she was able to speak, the loving grandmother said:
"No, my young brave, not so! You must not mourn for your first offering. Wash your face and then we will go."
The boy obeyed, submitted Ohitika to Wacoota with a smile, and walked off with his grandmother and Wahchewin.
The boy and his grandmother descended the bank, following a tortuous foot-path until they reached the water's edge. Then they proceeded to the mouth of an immense cave, some fifty feet above the river, under the cliff. A little stream of limpid water trickled down from a spring within the cave. The little watercourse served as a sort of natural staircase for the visitors. A cool, pleasant atmosphere exhaled from the mouth of the cavern. Really it was a shrine of nature, and it is not strange that it was so regarded by the tribe.
A feeling of awe and reverence came to the boy. "It is the home of the Great Mystery," he thought to himself; and the impressiveness of his surroundings made him forget his sorrow.
Very soon Wahchewin came with some difficulty to the steps. She placed the body of Ohitika upon the ground in a life-like position and again left the two alone.
As soon as she disappeared from view, Uncheedah, with all solemnity and reverence, unfastened the leather strings that held the four small bundles of paints and one of tobacco, while the filled pipe was laid beside the dead Ohitika.
She scattered paints and tobacco all about. Again they stood a few moments silently; then she drew a deep breath and began her prayer to the Great Mystery:
"O, Great Mystery, we hear thy voice in the rushing waters below us! We hear thy whisper in the great oaks above! Our spirits are refreshed with thy breath from within this cave. O, hear our prayer! Behold this little boy and bless him! Make him a warrior and a hunter as great as thou didst make his father and grandfather."
And with this prayer the little warrior had completed his first offering.

VII
THE GRAVE OF THE DOG
The full moon was just clear of the high mountain ranges when the game scout moved slowly homeward, well wrapped in his long buffalo robe, which was securely belted to his strong loins; his quiver tightly tied to his shoulders so as not to impede his progress.

As he emerged from the lowlands into the upper regions, he loomed up a gigantic figure against the clear, moonlit horizon. His picturesque foxskin cap with all its trimmings was incrusted with frost from the breath of his nostrils, and his lagging footfall sounded crisply. The distance he had that day covered was enough for any human endurance; yet he was neither faint nor hungry; but his feet were frozen into the psay, the snow-shoes, so that he could not run faster than an easy slip and slide. At last he reached the much-coveted point—the crown of the last ascent; and when he smelled fire and the savory odor of the jerked buffalo meat, it well-nigh caused him to waver! But he must not fail to follow the custom of untold ages, and give the game scout's wolf call before entering camp.

Accordingly he paused upon the highest point of the ridge and uttered a cry to which the hungry cry of a real wolf would have seemed but a coyote's yelp in comparison! Then it was that the rest of the buffalo hunters knew that their game scout was returning with welcome news; for the unsuccessful scout enters the camp silently.

In the meantime, the hunters at the temporary camp were aroused to a high pitch of excitement. Some turned their buffalo robes and put them on in such a way as to convert themselves into make-believe bison, and began to tread the snow, while others were singing the buffalo song, that their spirits might be charmed and allured within the circle of the camp-fires. The scout, too, was singing his buffalo bull song in a guttural, lowing chant as he neared the hunting camp. Within arrow-shot he paused again, while the usual ceremonies were enacted for his reception. This done, he was seated with the leaders in a chosen place.

"It was a long run," he said, "but there were no difficulties. I found the first herd directly north of here. The second herd, a great one, is northeast, near Shell Lake. The snow is deep. The buffalo can only follow their leader in their retreat."

"Hi, hi, hi!" the hunters exclaimed solemnly in token of gratitude, raising their hands heavenward and then pointing them toward the ground.

"Ho, kola! one more round of the buffalo-pipe, then we shall retire, to rise before daybreak for the hunt," advised one of the leaders. Silently they partook in turn of the long-stemmed pipe, and one by one, with a dignified "Ho!" departed to their teepees.

The scout betook himself to his little old buffalo teepee, which he used for winter hunting expeditions. His faithful Shunka, who had been all this time its only occupant, met him at the entrance as dogs alone know how to welcome a lifelong friend. As his master entered he stretched himself in his old-time way, from the tip of his tail to that of his tongue, and finished by curling both ends upward.

"Ho, mita Shunka, eat this; for you must be hungry!" So saying, the scout laid before his canine friend the last piece of his dried buffalo meat. It was the sweetest meal ever eaten by a dog, judging by his long smacking of his lips after he had swallowed it!

The hunting party was soon lost in heavy slumber. Not a sound could be heard save the gnawing of the ponies upon the cottonwood bark, which was provided for them instead of hay in the winter time.

When Wapashaw, the game scout, had rolled himself in his warm buffalo robe and was sound asleep, his faithful companion hunter, the great Esquimaux wolf dog, silently rose and again stretched himself, then stood quiet for a moment as if meditating. It was clear that he knew well what he had planned to do, but was considering how he should do it without arousing any suspicion of his movements. This is a dog's art, and the night tricks and marauding must always be the joy and secret of his life!

Softly he emerged from the lodge and gave a sweeping glance around to assure him that there were none to spy upon him. Suspiciously he sniffed the air, as if to ascertain whether there could be any danger to his sleeping master while he should be away.

Up the long ascent he trotted in a northerly direction, yet not following his master's trail. He was large and formidable in strength, combining the features of his wild brothers of the plains with those of the dogs who keep company with the red men. His jet-black hair and sharp ears and nose appeared to immense advantage against the spotless and jewelled snow, until presently his own warm breath had coated him with heavy frost.

After a time Shunka struck into his master's trail and followed it all the way, only taking a short cut here and there when, by dog instinct, he knew that a man must go around such a point to get to his destination. He met many travellers during the night, but none had dared to approach him, though some few followed at a distance, as if to discover his purpose.

At last he reached Shell Lake, and there beheld a great gathering of the herds! They stood in groups, like enormous rocks, no longer black, but white with frost. Every one of them emitted a white steam, quickly frozen into a fine snow in the air.

Shunka sat upon his haunches and gazed. "Wough, this is it!" he said to himself. He had kept still when the game scout gave the wolf call, though the camp was in an uproar, and from the adjacent hills the wild hunters were equally joyous, because they understood the meaning of the unwonted noise. Yet his curiosity was not fully satisfied, and he had set out to discover the truth, and it may be to protect or serve his master in case of danger.

At daybreak the great dog meekly entered his master's rude teepee, and found him already preparing for the prospective hunt. He was filling his inside moccasins full of buffalo hair to serve as stockings, over which he put on his large buffalo moccasins with the hair inside, and adjusted his warm leggins. He then adjusted his snow-shoes and filled his quiver full of good arrows. The dog quietly lay down in a warm place, making himself as small as possible, as if to escape observation, and calmly watched his master.

Soon all the hunters were running in single file upon the trail of the scout, each Indian closely followed by his trusty hunting dog. In less than two hours they stood just back of the low ridge which rounded the south side of Shell Lake. The narrow strip of land between its twin divisions was literally filled with the bison. In the gulches beyond, between the dark lines of timber, there were also scattered groups; but the hunters at once saw their advantage over the herd upon the peninsula.

"Hechetu, kola! This is well, friends!" exclaimed the first to speak. "These can be forced to cross the slippery ice and the mire around the springs. This will help us to get more meat. Our people are hungry, and we must kill many in order to feed them!"

"Ugh, he is always right! Our dogs must help us here. The meat will be theirs as well as ours," another added.

"Tosh, kola! The game scout's dog is the greatest Shunka of them all! He has a mind near like that of a man. Let him lead the attack of his fellows, while we crawl up on the opposite side and surround the buffalo upon the slippery ice and in the deceitful mire," spoke up a third. So it was agreed that the game scout and his Shunka should lead the attack.

"Woo, woo, woo!" was the hoarse signal from the throat of the game scout; but his voice was drowned by the howling and barking of the savage dogs as they made their charge. In a moment all was confusion among the buffalo. Some started this way, others that, and the great mass swayed to and fro uncertainly. A few were ready to fight, but the snow was too deep for a counterattack upon the dogs, save on the ice just in front of them, where the wind had always full sweep. There all was slippery and shining! In their excitement and confusion the bison rushed upon this uncertain plain.

Their weight and the momentum of their rush carried them hopelessly far out, where they were again confused as to which way to go, and many were stuck in the mire which was concealed by the snow, except here and there an opening above a spring from which there issued a steaming vapor. The game scout and his valiant dog led on the force of canines with deafening war-cries, and one could see black heads here and there popping from behind the embankments. As the herd finally swept toward the opposite shore, many dead were left behind. Pierced by the arrows of the hunters, they lay like black mounds upon the glassy plain.

It was a great hunt! "Once more the camp will be fed," they thought, "and this good fortune will help us to reach the spring alive!"

A chant of rejoicing rang out from the opposite shore, while the game scout unsheathed his big knife and began the work which is ever the sequel of the hunt—to dress the game; although the survivors of the slaughter had scarcely disappeared behind the hills.

All were busily skinning and cutting up the meat into pieces convenient for carrying, when suddenly a hunter called the attention of those near him to an ominous change in the atmosphere.

"There are signs of a blizzard! We must hurry into the near woods before it reaches us!" he shouted.

Some heard him; others did not. Those who saw or heard passed on the signal and hurried toward the wood, where others had already arranged rude shelters and gathered piles of dry wood for fuel.

Around the several camp-fires the hunters sat or stood, while slices of savory meat were broiled and eaten with a relish by the half-starved men. But the storm had now fairly enveloped them in whirling whiteness. "Woo, woo!" they called to those who had not yet reached camp. One after another answered and emerged from the blinding pall of snow. At last none were missing save the game scout and his Shunka!

The hunters passed the time in eating and telling stories until a late hour, occasionally giving a united shout to guide the lost one should he chance to pass near their camp.

"Fear not for our scout, friends!" finally exclaimed a leader among them. "He is a brave and experienced man. He will find a safe resting-place, and join us when the wind ceases to rage." So they all wrapped themselves in their robes and lay down to sleep.

All that night and the following day it was impossible to give succor, and the hunters felt much concern for the absent. Late in the second night the great storm subsided.

"Ho, ho! Iyotanka! Rise up!" So the first hunter to awaken aroused all the others.

As after every other storm, it was wonderfully still; so still that one could hear distinctly the pounding feet of the jack-rabbits coming down over the slopes to the willows for food. All dry vegetation was buried beneath the deep snow, and everywhere they saw this white-robed creature of the prairie coming down to the woods.

Now the air was full of the wolf and coyote game call, and they were seen in great numbers upon the ice.

"See, see! the hungry wolves are dragging the carcasses away! Harken to the war-cries of the scout's Shunka! Hurry, hurry!" they urged one another in chorus.

Away they ran and out upon the lake; now upon the wind-swept ice, now upon the crusted snow; running when they could, sliding when they must. There was certainly a great concourse of the wolves, whirling in frantic circles, but continually moving toward the farther end of the lake. They could hear distinctly the hoarse bark of the scout's Shunka, and occasionally the muffled war-whoop of a man, as if it came from under the ice.

As they approached nearer the scene they could hear more distinctly the voice of their friend, but still as it were from underground. When they reached the spot to which the wolves had dragged two of the carcasses of the buffalo, Shunka was seen to stand by one of them, but at that moment he staggered and fell. The hunters took out their knives and ripped up the frozen hide covering the abdominal cavity. It revealed a warm nest of hay and buffalo hair in which the scout lay, wrapped in his own robe!

He had placed his dog in one of the carcasses and himself in another for protection from the storm; but the dog was wiser than the man, for he kept his entrance open. The man lapped the hide over and it froze solidly, shutting him securely in. When the hungry wolves came Shunka promptly extricated himself and held them off as long as he could; meanwhile, sliding and pulling, the wolves continued to drag over the slippery ice the body of the buffalo in which his master had taken refuge. The poor, faithful dog, with no care for his own safety, stood by his imprisoned master until the hunters came up. But it was too late, for he had received more than one mortal wound.

As soon as the scout got out, with a face more anxious for another than for himself, he exclaimed:

"Where is Shunka, the bravest of his tribe?"

"Ho, kola, it is so, indeed; and here he lies," replied one sadly.

His master knelt by his side, gently stroking the face of the dog.

"Ah, my friend; you go where all spirits live! The Great Mystery has a home for every living creature. May he permit our meeting there!"

At daybreak the scout carried him up to one of the pretty round hills overlooking the lake, and built up around him walls of loose stone. Red paints were scattered over the snow, in accordance with Indian custom, and the farewell song was sung.

Since that day the place has been known to the Sioux as Shunkahanakapi—the Grave of the Dog.

THE END

GLOSSARY OF INDIAN WORDS

1. Be-day-wah´-kan-ton, lake-dwellers.
2. Cha-tan´-na, fourth son.
3. chin´-to, certainly.
4. Che-ton´-skah, white hawk.
5. Chank-pay´-yu-hah, carries the club.
6. coo´-wah, come here!
7. ha-nah´-kah-pee, grave.
8. he-yu´-pee-yay, come all of you!
9. hay´-chay-tu, it is well.
10. Hah-kay´-dah, the last-born.
11. he-nah´-kah-gah, the owl.
12. Kah-po´-se-yah, Light Lodges (a band of Sioux).
13. Ko´-lah, friend.
14. Man-kah´-to, blue earth.
15. Mah-to´, bear.
16. Mah-to´-sap-ah, black bear.
17. Mah-pee´-to-pah, four heavens.
18. Me-ne-yah´-tah, beside the water.
19. Me-chink´-shee, my son.
20. Nak-pah´, ears (of an animal).
21. O-o´-pay-han´-skah, bluebird.
22. o-hit´-e-kah, brave.
23. shun´kah, dog.
24. Sna´-na, rattle.
25. shunk-to´-kay-chah, wolf.
26. She-cho´-kah, robin.

27   Shun´-kah-skah, white dog.
28   tee´-pee, tent.
29   tak-chah´, deer.
30   to-kee´, well, well!
31   Ta-tee´-yo-pah, her door.
32   Un-chee´-dah, grand-mother.
33   u-tu´-hu, oak.
34   wa-kan´, holy, wonderful.
35   Wah-coo´-tay, shooter.
36   Wah-pay´-ton, dweller among the leaves.
37   Wah-chee´-win, dancing woman.
38   Wee-ko´, beautiful woman.
39   Wa-doo´-tah, scarlet.
40   we´-yan-nah, little woman.
41   We-no´-nah, first-born girl.
42   Wah-be-day´, orphan.
43   Zee-zee´-wee, yellow woman.

Freeriver Community

Freeriver is a community project working to create a place for people to visit and potentially live, long-term, in peace, free from the normal stresses of modern life.

We aim to provide a place where people can spend time discovering themselves and discovering nature. We aim to focus on creativity, health and wellbeing. We plan to provide events and classes for people in the local area and enhance the community.

Please visit our website for more details

www.freerivercommunity.com
freerivercommunity@hotmail.com

www.freerivercommunity.com

This book is in the public domain as the author died over 70 years ago and also the original was first published before 1923. No persons, organisation or establishment accept any ownership, liability or responsibility for the content of this book as it is in the public domain. Every attempt has been made to present you with an accurate version of the text, however there may be very subtle differences in text type, punctuation etc due to the editing process.

Charles Alexander Eastman (February 19, 1858 – January 8, 1939)

Any profits generated from the sale of this book will go towards the Freeriver Community project, a project designed to promote harmonious community living and well-being in the world. To learn more about the Freeriver project please visit the website - www.freerivercommunity.com

Made in the USA
Monee, IL
02 August 2020